# Miss Vee and the Lecherous Lawyer

ISBN: 978-988688-44-2
Sensitivity editing by: Cait Gordon, Dynamic Canvas Inc.
Cover by Nathan Frechette, Renaissance Press

Dedication:

To my lovely mother, who always had faith in me

To my husband who is both amazing and supportive

To my editor, Cait Gordon and my cover designer, Nathan Frechette who were instrumental in the creation you hold in your hands,

And most of all, to my own Miss Vee, without you, there would be no book

# Chapter One

"Your destination is ahead on the right. The route guidance is now ended."

The digitized British voice sounded loud in the silence. Jaqi eased up to the red light and glanced at me.

"You alright, Vee?"

I nodded, staring out the passenger window at the stately Victorian homes. Most had been converted to offices, but a few still had families living in them.

Smiths Falls had always been a pretty town. Even though I'd been gone over twenty years, it looked unchanged. A town time forgot.

The familiar streets only added to my misery.

"Can we just go to the hotel?"

(That Morning)

I WAS HAVING A GREAT time yard sale-ing by the retirement home. I'd found a gorgeous Royal Albert teacup and saucer for only five dollars! As I wandered through the painstakingly manicured yard, sorely tempted by a dark rose twin sweater set, I stopped dead in my tracks after spotting a large glass sculpture on the table before me. A woman bumped into me from behind and muttered an apology I barely heard. The *objet d'art* had captured all of my attention.

5

Orange and olive-green clouds floated within a clear glass base with a bright yellow twist swirling around them like a stream of tinkle. Not that I could think of any colors that would make it more acceptable as fashionable decor. It stood on a small round pedestal, swelling into a great round belly, then narrowed quickly to a cone on top. Sort of like a mushroom that hasn't opened yet, but taller.

I eased my way past the candlesticks and fake flowers, until I stood in front of the tired, middle-aged woman manning the cash box. I had no idea how to ask for the *objet*.

So, I pointed down the table from her a little and raised one eyebrow. She flushed so red, I worried about her blood pressure. Clearly, I didn't need to ask if she knew what it was.

"My mother bought it in 1969. She thought it was *avant garde.*" She smiled at me, obviously hoping I'd drop the topic.

I barked laughter—that was so much like my mother, bu, bu*ng something with no idea what it was, then claiming it was art.* My Aunt Bee, now, she would have not only recognized what it was, she also would have bought the thing as gift for my mother. Bee is where I got my sense of humor, not to mention my nickname. I'm Victoria Rose Lilley, and my aunt and I still share a love of antiques and '50s fashion that knows no bounds. My friends call me Vee. Bee calls me her flower child.

"Tell you what, Hun. I'll pay you four bucks for it, if you knock down the price of that sweater set." I knew that meant I was getting the coffee table conversation-starter for free, but beggars can't be choosers, and she really wanted that thing gone.

She hastily agreed and wrapped the sweater set around the glass to protect it. I giggled my way home. Should I just quietly set this curiosity on the mantle to see if my roommates said anything? Or should I hide it in my closet? I didn't really want this piece; it just struck me as so funny in the yard sale of a ninety-year-old woman's things.

So, of course, it was going right on the mantle.

THE HOTEL WAS BOXY and gray, and it had a weird restaurant. Badly as I wanted a drink, I didn't feel like chancing one at a place called the Samurai Cowboy. The place was a mix of old Japan and the Wild West.

The owners must have been high as kites to come up with that combo,

Lucia and I peered through the door when we checked in, and I swear my eyes nearly fell out of my head. It was a kind of Chinese-western chic. What on Earth would you call that? Either way, I hated it, but I hated everything right now.

Lucia glanced around, a smile tugging at the corner of her mouth. She mouthed, "I love it." I tried to scowl, but her eyes were shining with laughter, and I couldn't stay grumpy at my best friend.

So, I took a real look around this time. The lucky money cat at the cash register was wearing a tiny purple cowboy hat with a neon green cord. Ridiculous—and funny as hell. I grinned despite myself.

There were horse bridles and photos of cowboys on the walls and large, paper umbrellas hanging from the rafters. An almost life-size picture of John Wayne as a Samurai hung in a place of pride opposite the street door.

The waiter wore a short, red silk kimono with black jeans and cowboy boots, grinning good-naturedly when he saw us. A steer was embroidered over his heart. I just raised my eyebrow at him.

He shrugged. "The partners couldn't agree. So, we have basically two menus. You can order off both, if you like."

I decided I was neither brave enough nor drunk enough. I was also far too tense to go to sleep, so I split the difference and went for a walk.

Lucia came with me, leaving her girlfriend Jaqi to settle into our room.

I guess the town had changed a lot in the twenty years since I last paid attention. My favorite coffee shop had become a big chain one, whose coffee I found too strong and bitter. The German pub was gone; an art gallery dedicated to the history of the small town had taken its place. That might be worth looking into.

Smiths Falls had a surprisingly dramatic past, from being a stop on the Underground Railroad during slavery, to being a stop on the liquor route during prohibition. Not to mention ghosts, murders, Americans coming up to summer homes and bringing their slaves with them.

Yes, it was both a place of slavery and a light-post on the escape route. I idly wondered how many summer folk lost slaves while they were here on vacation.

Lucia and I turned away from the Rideau River, looking for a nice place for a pint or two. Maybe later I'd be willing to try Chinese-western cuisine. Or at least a martini with a paper umbrella.

Jaqi had agreed to take a few days off from writing to be with me. She'd met my family...'nuff said.

Jaqi was a popular mystery writer, drawing on both her Black and Mohawk heritage for her books. All three of us shared a townhome in Orleans, a family-oriented suburb of Ottawa, Canada's capital. It felt a bit crowded, but it worked.

Luci and I followed the road around to a picturesque bridge over the Rideau Canal.

Yes, we had both a Rideau River and a Rideau Canal. Plus, Smiths Falls is situated in the Rideau Valley. All of them were simply called The Rideau. We were forever losing tourists.

Speaking of, we stopped to watch the ducks cluster around a group of tourists waiting for the ghost tour at old Watson's Mill. It had a tragic past so it must be haunted, right?

We turned our backs on them and headed for the city center. It had changed quite a bit since I grew up here, but not so much that it wasn't familiar. The Kilt & Castle was gone, replaced by The Viking Hoard, still a restaurant, and still open late for live music. But I was looking for a quieter place.

By the time we reached the pie wedge, an odd triangular building about two yards wide at one end and 20 at the other, I could see a cheerful sign with blue and white *fleurs-de-lis*. The Bun Journee. I grinned; I do love a good food-related pun. *Bon journée* is French for good morning, and it was a cafe. Unless the food was terrible, it was my new favorite coffee shop.

The bell over the door played a happy-sounding jingle as we pushed our way into the cinnamon and vanilla shop. I don't mean just the scent; the cafe was painted like a cinnamon bun. It looked amazing. A soft creamy white ceiling with scattered drops of reddish-brown seemed to float over blended caramel and beige walls that included a wide stripe of the same reddish brown. The red and white tiled floor resembled a waxy paper wrapper, and indeed, it matched the dishes and napkins.

I was in love.

While I'd been gawking around, Luci had hurried to the glass cases, practically drooling on them. I came up behind her, intending to tease her, but my mouth dried at the sight of all of the pastries. Lemon bars, eclairs, Danishes with their fresh fruit spilling out, and of course, cinnamon buns. Bee's favorite was there, too, and I wondered if she ever came in for a tea and an almond croissant.

My breath hitched as I realized, again, that she was dead. I had somehow forgotten while I was showing Luci around town, but now the grief settled on me like lead blanket. Nothing looked appetizing anymore.

As if she felt my mood change, Luci turned to me. Her soft brown eyes were sympathetic under her curly black bangs, and her full mouth pouted a little. Or maybe not. It was a round Cupid's bow on the bottom and usually looked pouty, but the sexy kind, not the spoiled brat kind.

"Are you okay, Victoria? Do you want to stay or go?" She had one hand curled possessively over the glass case; I knew she wanted to stay. So, I forced a smile and pointed at the almond croissant.

"I'll have one of those, and do you have that tea with cinnamon and oranges?"

The man behind the counter was deliciously cute; too bad he was also about half my age and wearing a wedding ring. The adorable ones were always taken.

"Yes, we do. I brought it in special for one of my favorite customers; she can't get enough of it." He paused in thought as he pulled out my croissant. "In fact, this is what she ordered every time she came in." He frowned.

Luci's voice was hushed as she asked him if the woman's name was Beatrice Lilley.

He smiled widely, nodding. "Yes, do you know her? I haven't seen her in a couple weeks, I'm getting really worried."

"She died," I whispered, my voice harsh. It was too much, and I dropped into the nearest chair, big ugly tears spilling. I'd never been a pretty, delicate crier, more like a hysterical fruit bat. I yanked at a couple of napkins to dry my eyes, and the whole silver contraption went spinning off of the table.

(Ottawa)

THE LETTER WAS FROM Smiths Falls, from an estate lawyer.

My Aunt Bee lived in Smiths Falls. So did my mother and most of my family, but Bee mattered most to me.

I turned the letter over and over in my hands, my heart sinking and somehow in my throat at the same time.

*Mr. D. Snapper, Estate Lawyer.* Plain ivory stationery, no crest or printed labels. It was hand written. I had never heard of him.

I'll admit I was scared to open it. What if it was about Bee, the one person in my family who truly understood me? What if it was my mother? We weren't getting along since I underwent the "change," but I still had some hope of fixing the broken relationship.

As long as I didn't open it, it remained Schrodinger's letter. Equal chances of good news and bad. Neither until I opened it. Who am I kidding; no good news ever comes in a letter from an estate lawyer.

So, I slid my heavily-varnished thumbnail under the flap and slit it open. A single folded paper fell onto the table. I reached for it slowly, tears already gathering in my eyes. Bee was in her nineties, and I hadn't heard from her in a couple of weeks.

I looked over the letter; it said that Mr. Snapper extended his deepest condolences on the death of my aunt. I couldn't see to read anymore, the words all blurred together. I felt someone pull the letter from my hand. Lucia's voice softly told me how sorry she was. I hadn't heard them come in. I forgot completely about my ugly *objet d'art* on the table beside me. I'd forgotten to place it on the living room mantle.

Bee couldn't be dead. I'd just seen her about...six weeks ago. I didn't want to hear Luci's condolences. It made things real.

I dried my tears and had a sip of the strong tea that had somehow appeared at my elbow. I held out my hand and Jaqi dropped the letter back into it. I could tell by the sad look in her dark eyes that she'd read it.

My Aunt Bee had died nearly a month ago, the funeral was over. My grief turned to anger in a heartbeat.

How could my mother not tell me? She knew how close we were. To not invite me to the funeral, or even let me know, hurt almost as much as the fact of Bee's death. Had she died in hospital? Did she ask for me?

The reading of the will was tomorrow (thanks for the heads-up, Mr. Snapper) and I was named as a beneficiary. I would certainly have a few words with my mother after the reading. I could hear Jaqi calmly making a hotel reservation for two nights for three people.

"Jaqi, you aren't going, are you? You have a deadline." She waved a hand to shush me and continued talking to the hotel. Lucia gently pulled me to my feet, pushing me toward my room.

"You need to pack for a few days, Vee. There will be paperwork, and you'will want to spend time with your family, no?"

"No. Except my mother. Her I definitely want to talk to." But there was no weight to my voice, no hint of the anger pounding through me.

"Of course you want to talk with your mom, such a terrible thing."

"Yes, she is." But Luci's soft Spanish accent and girlish voice stopped me from telling her anything. She was a sweetheart, through and through. Her big, doe-like, dark eyes simmered with tears of sympathy as she sat me in my rocker and opened the closet doors to find my suitcase.

THANK GODS WE WERE the only people in the Bun Journee this close to closing. Luci wrapped her arms around my shoulders from behind, laying her head atop mine.

The man pulled out a chair next to me and grasped my hand as he sat down. He didn't even glance at the mess I'd made. "I'm so sorry, was she a relative?"

I nodded, "My aunt, but she was more of a mother to me, has been since I was five." I gulped, trying to stop ugly-crying in front of this poor man. But when I looked up, tears shone in his eyes—his hypnotic, blue eyes with a dark ring around the iris. I lost myself staring at them for a moment, then shook my head.

"Thank you, I'm sorry for..." My voice trailed off. He squeezed my fingers gently.

"No, I'm sorry for bringing it up. I didn't mean to hurt you. I guess you reminded me of her." He smiled and rose, heading for the counter as the bell over the door rang.

He served them quickly, making their order to-go, telling them that he was closing early for a family emergency. Then he brought our order to the table and locked the door, turning his cheery OPEN sign off. He sat back down in the chair and leaned forward, his eyes meeting mine.

"I wish I'd known, I'd have gone to the funeral. She was a wonderful woman, so warm and funny; she was a real pip." He smiled, the corner of his mouth tilting up, revealing a deep dimple. "She called herself that. Said it had been a real compliment back in her day."

I smiled, "It was. And she certainly was."

"When is the memorial? Maybe I could cater it. For free. She was my favorite customer and a friend." He finished quietly.

I put my hand over his. "I wish I knew. It's probably over. My family didn't bother to tell me."

His mouth dropped open like I'd tied a barbell to his chin.

By the time we got back to the hotel, it was after nine and colored lights were shining through the restaurant windows. It almost looked welcoming. Except for the neon outline of a sumo wrestler in cowboy boots above the door.

The girl behind the front desk waved at me as we entered the lobby. "Are you, um, Miss Lilley?"

I nodded and walked over to her, taking the folded piece of hot pink paper she held out.

As I read it, she muttered, "Your, um, mother called. She said to call her back right away."

That was almost word for word what the note said, except that it included a phone number. And no ums. The same number she'd had since us kids were born. Like I'd forget it.

I noticed Jaqi was asleep beside her laptop and tried to be quiet, but there are no quiet talks with my mother. Her yelling over the phone woke Jaqi and made Luci's eyes go wide. My mother was a very creative woman when it came to cursing. At least in private. In public you'd swear butter wouldn't melt in her mouth, whatever that means.

"Until you come to your senses there's nothing for you here. Stop pretending you're better than us."

I nearly choked, torn between laughing at the absurdity and snorting in disbelief. I'm pretending I'm better than her?

"Well, I got a letter saying I'm in the will. And I want to be there. I want to say goodbye."

By the time I got off the phone to one last, "Well, you do what you want, you always do anyway," Jaqi had opened a bottle of wine and poured it into the three paper coffee cups that came with the room.

I gulped it down, wheezed for a moment, then held out my cup for more.

Soon, the second bottle was empty, and I felt a bit better. My mother wanted me there in a suit, so I'd wear a suit. Lucia had packed a lovely lavender, Chanel-style skirt-suit with cream heels. I don't remember owning those shoes, but I was too drunk to care. I had white gloves and nude pantyhose in the suitcase along with a soft white blouse. I would be stunning.

The family appointment was at ten the next morning, and I would need a good breakfast to avoid a hangover, so I changed into my nightie, a cute granny gown with kittens all over it. It had been a gift from Bee. I always smiled when I wore it; this was love in velvety flannel.

# Chapter Two

My head felt like something had burrowed through my skull and died in my mouth. Bleh!

After showering and brushing my teeth, I felt a bit less zombie and a bit more human. As Lucia zipped into the washroom, I yelled, "I'll be downstairs having coffee!"

Through the door I heard her surprised voice. "In the restaurant?"

I muttered, "Yeah, I'm so not ready for outside."

The coffee wasn't horrible. In fact, it was pretty good, though that might be more need than actual taste. And the same waiter was there, smiling when he saw me.

"Feeling strong enough to brave a Chinese omelet with gravy?"

My stomach tried to twist, but I forced it to be still. I even smiled at him.

"How about a normal western omelet and a gallon of coffee? I have three others joining me, and this little carafe won't be enough."

"Not a problem." He picked up the small carafe and shook it, hearing it slosh. He topped up my cup before saying "I'll be right back with a family size."

I might just survive the next hour, bless him.

15

KAREY AND HER SONS arrived before the girls. I felt a wash of love as I hugged my baby sister. Then I heard sniggering. I can't imagine how my sweet, quiet sister ended up with such jerks for kids. Actually, I can, it was her jerk of a husband. The one who decided that twin boys were too much like work and ran off with another woman. He came back when they were eleven and forced my sister into a shared custody agreement because "knowing their father was important."

But that's none of my business; I just deal with the whole family as best I can.

Karey shushed them with a frown and sat beside me. The boys—thirty-year-old men, actually—remained standing. The better to heap their scorn on me, I guess. So, I paid them the worst insult I knew. I ignored them.

Karey and I chatted, catching up on the little bits of news of daily life until our food arrived. By then Jaqi and Luci had arrived, and we were on the second pot of coffee.

Elliot and Robert were starting to look peeved that no-one was paying any attention to them. They were especially angry at Jaqi and Luci, both of whom ignored them completely as they chatted while getting to know Karey.

"You know, I've just realized how much I miss you. I should never have let Mom keep me from visiting."

Karey glanced at me, then lowered her eyes as a slight flush rose to her neck. "Maybe it's best you don't. Visit, I mean. Mom's blood pressure..."

She trailed off as I paled. "Even you?" I whispered.

Robert laughed, "Nobody wants you around, ya freak." Elliot laughed with him as Karey flushed in shame.

I turned to face Karey, feeling betrayed. "Do you agree with him? Do you want me to stay away?"

"No, yes... just until Mom is gone, maybe. I have to live with her. She needs me."

I nodded, not feeling any better. I just finished my coffee and waived for the bill.

"We'd better get going or we'll be late. Mother would love that, one more thing to criticize."

"Fran-Victoria, that's not fair. This was such a shock." She waved at my lavender Jackie O' suit.

"Karey, it was a shock five years ago. And she was warned it was happening."

"She misses her son."

"But not me." Karey opened her mouth to explain but shut it without saying anything. She waved at the boys, who had sat at the next table when standing there being ignored had become boring.

Time to see the lawyer.

OF COURSE, JAQI COULDN'T leave her writing behind; she brought a notebook and pen. I swear, that girl could no more blow off a day's writing than I could sprout wings and fly to the lawyer's office.

It would take a national emergency to get her to miss a day, and even then, I think she'd send the soldiers running away with their tails between their legs.

Lucia and I sat silently in the waiting area. I suppose you could count Jaqi in that, too, except for the scratching of her pen. It was a typical lawyer's office, I suppose, all dark wood and leather, very masculine. I hadn't slept well, and the stuffy air and classical music had my eyes drifting closed. My thoughts were just starting to buzz softly with weird dreaminess when the door slammed open and nearly sent me out of my seat like a scalded cat.

"What on Earth are you wearing?" The voice was loud and nasal. My Mother. "Frank, what has gotten into you?"

Lucia glanced around, then stared her right in the eye. "What Frank are you talking to?"

"That freak you're sitting beside," Robert said. "Aren't you worried you're going to catch something? You'd be better off sitting with me, sweetheart." He sat on a loveseat and patted his lap.

I gazed at him calmly and sniffed, like Queen Elizabeth when she's disgusted but too polite to say anything. Then I rubbed my forehead and looked away, already feeling the tightening of a tension headache behind my eyes.

Fortunately, the inner door opened, and the secretary came out to smile at us.

"Mr. Snapper is ready for you now."

Her smile faltered a bit as Elliot whistled at her, but she kept her head up. Good for her.

She held the door for us as Lucia and I made our way over. The "boys" made it to the door first and motioned at us, saying, "Ladies first." I smiled in relief; maybe they had changed for the better. But as I went to follow Lucia and Jaqi into the inner office, Robert blocked the door, his upraised arm releasing a boggy, sweaty smell. I could feel my nose-hairs curl.

"I said ladies, Victor-Victoria. Not whatever you think you are." They crowded through the door, needlessly pushing me out of their way. The secretary grabbed my arm to help me with my balance. I smiled at her, and in my sweetest give-you-diabetes voice said, "Fuck them."

She bit her lip to hide a smile and closed the door behind us.

Mr. Snapper, like the fish he's named after, had a weak, damp handshake. He paused for a moment, looking me up and down, and I held back a sigh.

Surprisingly, he took my hands in his and leaned in to kiss both of my cheeks like a Frenchman and murmured condolences into my ear.

He smiled at me and held my hands just a moment too long, when things shift from sympathy to creepy. When he finally returned to his desk, Lucia frowned at me.

"I do not trust him, he feels slippery, like a frog."

I nodded, he felt like that to me, too. Like he was playacting.

We waited about twenty minutes for the rest of the family to arrive. My Mother's other sister, Kay, was looking rough, hair falling out of her braid, eyes red from crying. My mother sniffed at me, as I had sniffed at my nephews. So, not Queen Elizabeth after all. I didn't have time to talk to her though, as Snapper dove right in, calling us to order like a board meeting.

Then, although he could have done it while we were waiting, he made a show of calling loudly for Miss Pineault for a dozen coffees, cream and sugar on the side.

We made small talk waiting for her to return from the convenience store in the lobby downstairs, then to ask how we took our coffees and serve them. I was getting twitchy under the constant stares from my family. Only Aunt Kay seemed sympathetic, my mother didn't even look in my direction. Lucia reached over to hold my hand.

Eventually, Snapple got down to business. He read all of the usual sound mind and body things, and that the will had been modified five years ago. I gasped at the date— the day I'd come home from my surgery.

The will had only a few surprises. Not the donations to the library, or the Gay-Straight Alliance, or the place that helps homeless LGBTQ+ kids. I'd expected that. No, it was the amounts.

Aunt Bee had been far richer than I'd thought. Why had she stayed in that tiny little war house all of these years? She could have lived anywhere: Paris, Florida, even Ottawa, so she'd be closer to me.

She was also a bit vindictive.

She left her sisters fifty grand each. My sister, Karey, got thirty grand.

I was so shocked that I missed the next few bequests until Robert and Elliot started swearing. Karey asked the lawyer to read that again, so I got to hear what all of the uproar was about. And I started laughing like a fool. Oh, my Aunt Bee could see through people all right. No flies on that dear lady.

"To my great-nephews Robert and Elliot Sanders, I leave the bare legal limit needed to prevent a lawsuit to overturn my will. I have always detested you, as you always did me, and leave you this five thousand each, only under the advisement of my lawyer. As you have always done the bare minimum of what is necessary in life, I give you the bare minimum necessary in death." I howled with laughter. Gods, I loved that woman. They had always despised her, and she knew it.

I wiped away tears. Even if I had gotten nothing in the will, this was the greatest gift she could have given me. Lucia fought back a smile as she met my eyes. I reached for my purse, ready to leave, but Lucia pulled me back down, I had to stay until the end.

I nodded but left my purse on my lap. Snaffle smiled at me like he thought I was a supermodel. Ew. I'd rather the honest disgust of my subhuman nephews.

But I smiled politely and nodded that I was ready to hear the rest. Unexpectedly, he pulled out a USB stick and plugged it into his laptop. He then swiveled it around so that the whole room could see the screen. It was Aunt Bee, dressed in her Sunday finest. She wore a sky-blue, slub silk suit with a pink blouse and a string of pink faux pearls. At least, I had always assumed they were fake. Maybe they weren't. She looked so adorable. I had to swallow around the lump in my throat and wipe my eyes again. I missed her already.

She stared owlishly at the camera for a moment, then smiled.

"I wanted to tell you this part in person, so to speak, so there could be no misunderstanding about my intent or my faculties.

To my dearest niece, Victoria Rose Lilley, I leave my house and all its contents, including the contents of the old writing desk and everything that pertains to them. You have always been such a lovely child; it was my privilege and pleasure to watch you bloom into the beautiful young woman you are now. And don't let those arseholes bully you, they already got more than they deserve. If I wanted them to have more, I'd have given it to them.

I'm going to miss everyone, but you most of all. All those holidays you came up to keep an old lady company, all those hot chocolates and cookies while watching terrible chick-flicks." She laughed, patting her pearl necklace. It was a habit I'd learned from her, and I deliberately moved my hand away from my own necklace.

"There's not much else to say. Go on to the house now and have a look around. You don't need to keep everything, feel free to redecorate, or even renovate. It's all yours now. Love you, girlie."

She blew a kiss at the screen and the lawyer clicked it off.

I just sat still for a moment, my hand creeping up to pat my necklace. She'd left me the house. I loved my room in Jaqi's house, but things could get tense with us all living in each other's pockets like we were. I knew that Jaqi and Lucia would like more time alone but felt guilty sending me out to the mall. The house was in Smiths Falls, but an hour wasn't too far to visit.

My thoughts were shattered when Elliot jumped up and started yelling. "Why does that pervert get the house? It's gotta be worth two-hundred grand."

My mother jumped in with "Now Frank, just because Beatrice left the house to you, doesn't mean you need to keep it. You could sell it and share the money with your family. She had some really nice antiques that must be wor—"

"Stop it! Just stop it!" I was yelling with tears roughening my voice. ""Why are you more upset about the money than the fact that she's dead?"

"Be reasonable. She was ninety-four, and she had a nice, long life."

"Reasonable? I'm heartbroken. I'd give all of it up to get one more visit with her, to be able to say goodbye!" I broke down in tears, and Lucia put her arms around me. I could feel her warmth and love surround me, and I drew a shuddering breath, immediately calming down. A vague memory of hugging Aunt Bee goodbye last month drifted into my mind.

Until my mother whispered hoarsely, "Frank, stop being so melodramatic, it's embarrassing." She smiled apologetically at the lawyer.

"If you want to give it all up, Frankie, I'll take it." Robert snarled from his side of the room.

Lucia rose to my defense, hissing like a wildcat. "*Her* name is Victoria. How can you be so hurtful to your own daughter?"

My mother sniffed, taking in Lucia's obviously Latina heritage. "Because I gave birth to a son. He'll always be Frank to me."

Suddenly, I was utterly exhausted. I sat, head bowed under the weight of family expectations and disappointment. I just wanted to go home. I tugged Lucia's hand to whisper to her to go get the car. She bit her lip but nodded and left.

Mr. Sniffer eventually got everyone shooed out of his office by agreeing to have everything ready to sign the next morning at eleven. He motioned at me to stay behind. I settled into my seat warily. I had a few minutes. I might as well hear him out. He pulled a chair up next to mine but sat in it sideways so that he could lay one arm along the back of my chair and place the other hand on my thigh. I carefully picked it up by the wrist, as if it were trash, and dropped it on his own leg.

"My dear Vicky—may I call you Vicky?"

"No." I felt so unlike myself, angry, disgusted, exhausted, and so cranky. I probably should have apologized, but I hate being called Vicky.

"Oh, er, of course. Miss Lilley." He smiled again. "Your Aunt asked me to give you the keys to the house immediately. I guess she felt you would stay there until everything is finalized."

"When will it all be done? Does it have to go through court or anything?"

"Of course, there's always paperwork. It's how we poor lawyers make our living." His eyes glowed a warm shit-brown, and he chuckled like he expected me to join in on the joke. When I didn't, he cleared his throat and told me to be there at nine and we'd get it all done before everyone else arrived.

I held my hand out for the keys, not speaking. They were heavier than I expected, a blocky square with her initial acting as the key-fob. A safety deposit box key hung among the keys to the front and back door and to her mint condition 60's convertible. Tears pricked my eyes, she hadn't been allowed to drive for more than a decade, but she loved that car. She had bought it new, washed it every Sunday and allowed neighborhood boys to use it at prom every year.

And now it was mine.

Snapper reached back to his desk and picked up an envelope. He held it towards me but moved it out of reach as I went to take it. He smiled, holding it out again. What was he? Twelve?

I refused to play and crossed my arms, giving him a raised eyebrow. After a moment, he caved and handed me the envelope.

What a goober.

I should have let him keep it as his unoccupied hand drifted onto my thigh again. I grabbed his wrist, but this time he wouldn't let me move it, pressing his damp fingers into my leg. He'd better hope his sweat didn't stain my skirt.

"My dearest Miss Lilley, do you believe in love at first sight? I just feel so drawn to you. Like a honey-bee to a frail beautiful rose."

"More like a moth to a bug-zapper. I am so too much for you to handle." I didn't enjoy his flirting, but a lady never tells a gentleman to sod off. Unless he proves himself not a gentleman.

Which he did a moment later. He managed to slip his fingers under my skirt as he leaned in far enough for me to smell his coffee-stale breath.

"Please, come to lunch with me. I'll do anything to be in your company, my love." His fingers slid higher.

That was it. I don't have a clue what he thought he was doing but I have boundaries. And standards.

So, I used my strong forearm to force his hand off of my leg and out of my skirt. I may have twisted his wrist a little. He looked surprised and leaned back in his chair, pulling to get his hand back.

Watching him carefully in case he got touchy-feely again, I leaned slightly forward. Smiling widely, he leaned forward, too, reaching for my hands. Which I quickly pulled away.

"Dearest Vicky, Tell me how I can help you through this terrible time."

I wanted to tell him that stopping the predatory behavior would help, but my momma didn't raise no fools. But how to call him a greasy ape in a ladylike manner?

"My sweet lady, may I call you sweetheart?"

"Absolutely not!" I was so indignant that I nearly forgot what I was going to say. But I just gritted my teeth and kept to the matter at hand, so to speak.

"What type of lawyer would I need to set up a trust fund to donate to LGBTQ groups?" It wasn't what I'd meant to say, I'd meant to tell him off, but it was a lovely idea.

"Why would a lady like you want to donate to such people? They're..."

He fumbled for a word, and I picked his wrist up by two fingers and dropped it onto his own knee again.

"They are my people Mr. Shitter. Be careful what you say next."

"You're, you're..." His eyes widened and his face turned red as he snatched his hand back.

"I'm a trans woman, if that's what you're asking." I smiled and leaned closer, watching him back up. "I thought that you knew." I lowered my voice to its bass notes. "Where are you going, sweetheart?"

By now he was resting his butt on the edge of his desk, a good six feet away. It wasn't funny anymore, it was tiring. It was pathetic. I hate small towns.

No, I love small towns. I hate small minds. And lawyers. And small-minded lawyers.

The secretary walked in and paused at our tableau. Mr. Slutter leaning on the desk looking scared, me sitting in my chair looking utterly disgusted.

Her forehead wrinkled as she gazed at me.

I MADE IT DOWN TO THE lobby before realizing I had left my suit jacket on a chair. Peering out the glass doors, I saw no sign of Lucia, so I headed back to the elevator to go get it. I had zero desire to see that man again, but it was a Chanel.

As I slowly rose, I was glad not to be claustrophobic. The antique brass and leather were beautiful, but I could get upstairs faster by crawling.

The pinger didn't work, so the doors opened with only a slight clunk at the right floor. I guess Mr. Studmuffin and Miss Pinmedown didn't hear it, wrapped up as they were on her desk. I only caught a glimpse of her bare leg up in the air and him leaning over her, face in her boobs, and hit the close doors button hard enough to crack a nail.

*EW!* I did not need that mental image burned into the back of my retinas, but there it was.

I'd get my jacket tomorrow.

I had planned to go window shopping and check up on some of my formerly favorite places, but just wasn't in the mood.

I decided to drop by the Bun Journee for a light lunch; I wasn't up to heavy food. My family and Mr. Sneaky-hands had my stomach in knots.

Ben was behind the counter, ringing up a tray of pastries and coffee. He grinned when he saw me, a warm, welcoming sight on a miserable day. I couldn't help smiling back, though mine had far less wattage. He let his smile slip a little as tears filled my eyes. My snarly side pointed out that I was unlikely to be welcome here much longer if I cried every time I walked in.

"I'm sorry, I don't mean to scare off your customers."

I felt like a fool crying in front of a virtual stranger, but he didn't seem to mind. He led me to a chair and helped me sit. One of his hands covered mine gently, and his eyes warmed with sympathy.

"It's just my blood sugar"—I tried to wave him away—"I had an early breakfast."

He was having none of it. "Life is hard for people like us, isn't it? Especially in a small town."

"It's not that. Most people have been fine. It was the reading of Aunt Bee's will." I opened my purse to find a tissue, but he handed me a couple of napkins. It dawned on me that he had said *people like us*. "Are you trans?"

He smiled. "No, but we're openly gay, and it cost my husband a promotion last year." He tried to sound casual about it, but there was a thread of anger in his voice. Then he visibly pushed the anger away and squeezed my hand gently. "We fabulous people have to stick together."

He was so cute with his dark hair in short spikes and the dimple beside his generous mouth, I couldn't help but smile back at him. "Thank you; I don't know what came over me. I'd like to get lunch, if you don't mind?"

He grinned and said in the cutest French accent, "I shall fetch la mademoiselle un soup de jour, un sandwich pour la dejournée, et un café, oui?"

I laughed, if he had hoped to impress me or confuse me, he was out of luck. I lived in Ottawa, the most bilingual city ever. A soup and sandwich sounded good, but I'd already had enough coffee for today.

"Mais oui, Monsieur Les yeux bleu." I grinned when he blinked, though whether it was surprise at my grasp of French or my calling him Mr. Blue Eyes, I had no idea. "But make that an Earl Grey tea, please."

"Comme vous voulez, ma jolie dame!" *As you wish, my pretty lady.*

I smiled as he loped to the counter to put my tray together. I felt happy for the first time since arriving last night. I could feel my shoulders relax as I settled back into my chair.

Soon I had a lovely cup of tea, a hot bowl of tomato cheese bisque, a toasted tomato and chicken sandwich, and a flaky pastry with jam and whipped cream leaking from its many layers. And it was all delicious.

I ate every scrap and decided against licking the bowl. But if he delivered, all bets were off.

"HEY! WHAT ARE YOU DOING?"

He turned, and I recognized my nephew Robert. I was striding up to him when my sister ran out of Bee's yard after him. I turned to her for an explanation, but she avoided my gaze. She looked guilty as sin.

It was a good thing I'd decided to check on Bee's place or Lord knew what would have happened.

"Karey? What were you doing back there?"

"She was my great-aunt, too."

"No-one said she wasn't, but she left me the house, why were you both in the back yard?"

Robert curled his lip at me, "She left us some stuff. We were just trying to get it."

Karey waved her hand to shush him, and my suspicions grew. "If she left you *stuff,* why wasn't it in the will? Karey?"

Karey shook her head, then Robert growled, "She was old as Christ, maybe she forgot."

I growled in return, "Maybe she said exactly what she meant to say, and you were trying to break in and steal things that don't belong to you." I fished in my purse for my cell phone. I wouldn't really call the police on my sister, but I wanted her thick-headed son to get that this was serious.

Karey grabbed my arm and looked up at me, tears in her eyes that looked so much like mine. Hers were a muddier green, more hazel, but the shape and expressiveness were identical.

I melted a bit; Bee had left her high and dry when she left everything to me. I just didn't want Jughead to get his hands on Bee's beautiful antiques. He'd sell them for beer money. But I could share a bit with my sister, if she promised to keep them as heirlooms.

But just as I opened my mouth to offer her a share of Bee's things, she ruined her chances.

"Why do you insist on embarrassing us like this?"

"Like what?" I asked, my hackles rising.

She waved her hand dismissively at my outfit. "This! Dressing like a woman, we have to live here, you know. Mom is livid that you actually wore a skirt to the lawyer's."

"You look stupid." Robert offered and both of us glared at him. He shrugged, "Well, you do."

I took a deep breath, arguing on the street was not an option, not for me.

"Karey, do you remember how miserable I was here? I never fit in, always getting chased or beaten up? Do you?"

"Of course, but you were still a guy."

"No, everyone thought I *was* a guy. Now I'm living as the woman I am. That's what the bullies sensed about me, and why I hated myself. I was always a woman."

Robert snorted, and I tried to ignore the little shit.

"Frankie, I miss my big brother." She looked like she was about to cry, and I reached out to hold her. She was stiff as I put my arms around her, but she wasn't pushing me away.

"I'm still here, same person, same heart. All that's changed is my outside, and I was never a good-looking boy to begin with."

She snuffle-snorted, chuckling through her tears. "It's just such a big change, it's weird."

"No, sweetie, what's weird is being forced to be something I'm not because other people like it better. Would you spend your life trying to be a boy just because Dad wanted another son?"

"No, of course not." She looked at me, softly this time. I saw the light of understanding in her eyes. Small, but definitely a start.

"Karey, I'm happy for the first time in my life. I'm sixty years old, and I'm finally feeling at home in my own body. Can't you just be happy for me?"

She nodded, "I'll try. I didn't lose a big brother—I found a big sister."

She stared at her feet for a long moment before a smile crept slowly across her face. "Does this mean I get to teach you about nail polish and hairstyles?"

I grinned back, "Oh, Hun. Did you not see these nails?" I held up my long, perfectly shaped, petal pink nails for her to ooh and awe over. I tucked the broken one under my thumb. It would have spoiled the effect.

I SAT ALONE IN THE Samurai Cowboy nursing my second glass of white wine. I figured they couldn't really screw up pouring from a bottle, and I never liked those sugary, girlie drinks Chinese restaurants are famous for. Add a cowboy hat, and I didn't even want to think about it. Singapore whiskey sling. Bourbon flavored sake.

As I gestured for a refill, I realized that I'd better either slow down or eat something. It was only four-thirty, and my nose was already feeling numb. If I kept this up, someone would have to carry me upstairs.

I picked up the menu and flipped through it. Eggrolls were probably safe. The hot-dog fried rice hurt my head, but a nice bowl of soup might be good.

I waved at the waiter with a pink kimono and black 10-gallon hat. He came back with a smile, "Has the liquid courage prepared you to try the sweet and sour chicken fried steak?"

"No way, no how, no hope," I said with a shudder. He grinned and leaned in to whisper in my ear that he'd never tried it either. I giggled, which I *never* do. But the wine and the young cowboy's breath on my neck was too much for me.

I ordered the beef and vegetable soup and a pair of meat eggrolls. And another glass.

As I happily slurped this excellently spiced soup, my cell rang with a Native drumbeat. Jaqi.

"Hello sweetie," I said, " What's up?"

"Lucia says you're alone and we should be there. She says your family was *muy* Horrible. I could hear Lucia whispering in soft Spanish in the background. She must be livid.

"I'm having some soup and a glass of wine at the hotel restaurant." I tried to sound prim but hiccupped in the middle.

"*A* glass of wine?" She sounded amused. "Anyway, Luci wants us to keep you company.

The hotel was renovated from what was likely a warehouse, as it was boxy, really close to the Rideau River, and had parking for only a dozen cars. That meant that the sunset over the river was both blinding and beautiful. At least compared to the hotel, it was beautiful.

Luci flung an order for nachos to my pink cowboy as she swayed through the door on spiky-heeled boots. Her hips moved like a pirate ship on high seas, and her red leggings showed off her cute legs.

I sighed; she was adorable. If I were only she was single and twenty years older. Either way, the men in the bar sure noticed her and the waiter hopped to get her order.

Hands on her hips, one side of her lip caught between her teeth, she paused to stare me down. Luci was so cute in red and black, with that leather jacket fitted to perfection. She waved her hand in my face, and I scowled.

"What?"

"How much have you been drinking? And I thought you had wine."

I looked down at my hand holding a martini with a fragile curl of lemon peel in the bottom.

"It felt like three glasses of cheap wine had numbed my tongue enough that even their martini would taste good. It's actually not bad. Cheap vermouth, but what can you expect?"

She sat beside me. "How many?"

"This is my first, honest." She stared into my eyes and nodded. Our little human lie detector.

"You need food, soup is not enough, and you don't want to be near the creepy lawyer with a hangover. You'd be throwing yourself up on his shoes."

I smiled slightly at the image this raised. "Maybe then he'd keep his hands to himself."

She laughed: head tipped back showing her throat. The men in the room practically sighed like a wind through taut sails. Lucia noticed the men at a table near us staring, and leaned over to whisper to me.

"Look, Vee. They like you; they want to buy you a drink."

"I think they're looking at you." But I did lean around her to peek at the three young things in tight jeans and plaid shirts. "But I would do the one in the middle. Did you see those baby blues?"

The door opened and Jaqi sashayed in, a vision of elegance and strength.

"Psht, I'd do her." Lucia whispered loud enough to be heard at the bar. Several men snickered, then wilted under Jaqi's glare. I tried to stop giggling, but Jaqi was just so gorgeous when she was mad. Her clean, wide brow got two little lines between her eyebrows and her lips pursed up like she was about to blow you a kiss.

With her thick hair in a hundred braids with ribbons and beads woven in, she looked like a supermodel at five-eleven plus heels.

"What are you two doing?"

I straightened up, leaning only a little to one side. "Waiting for you, of course."

Jaqi smiled and sat down, "Vee, it's barely five o'clock, and you're drunk." She sounded shocked; she'd be clutching her pearls next. I peered closer at her chest. Her turquoise and copper beads, actually. Not pearls.

Lucia levered me upright, and I realized I'd been in danger of nose-planting in Jaqi's bosom. Okay, maybe the soup wasn't quite enough, and I *was* a wee bit drunk.

I smiled, "We should order supper. I have things to tell you."

Soon we had nachos, BBQ ribs, hot-dog fried rice (I was right, it was awful), and Chinese veggies in a garlic sauce. It sobered me up quickly, especially the fried rice. I delicately spit a mouthful into my lace-edged handkerchief and hid it in my purse.

Lucia winked at me and proceeded to eat a huge amount of the same rice. She loved it. Go figure.

As we slowed down, Jaqi wiped her mouth and leaned back in her seat.

"So, tell me what's going on that has you drinking before five o'clock."

I was going to say that nothing was bothering me, but she was right. I never drank before five. I leaned back to order my thoughts and take another sip of my martini.

"Oh, it was just the whole day, start to finish. Except for Benoit. He was sweet." I recounted what happened with the lawyer after Lucia left, and his tryst with the secretary, Miss Pineault. That led to meeting up with Karey at Bee's. Lucia huffed at the nerve of them trying to break in, and squeed when I told her about Benoit.

Robert walked in, trailed by Elliot. My face fell—the evening *had* been improving—I must've been a real jerk in a former life to get these two as family.

Before they could do more than sneer at us, Jaqi waved our waiter over.

"These two have been harassing Vee all day. Can something be done?"

The waiter, I really must get his name, practically frog-marched them to a table as far from us as he could. He bent over and said something and Elliot's face paled. I could see his lips compress into a line from here.

The waiter returned, and I read his nametag before I could forget. James, a nice name. He smiled at us and leaned in to speak quietly.

"Please enjoy your meal and drinks. Everything is on the house tonight.

I smiled up at him. "James, that is so kind of you, but I can't let you give us all of those drinks."

He smiled back. "You can and you will. You're too beautiful to have a jerk ruin your evening."

So, I did what he suggested, I settled back and enjoyed the rest of my second martini. Um...third martini?

# Chapter Three

The wine had made Luci's cheeks pink and her mood amorous. Once in the room, Jaqi grinned at her and stage-whispered, "No romance tonight—not in front of Vee."

Lucia turned to me, blushing a bit. I just rolled my eyes and kept to myself I'd heard them through the walls often enough. I sighed, slightly envious. They were so in love. I'd never been that certain, even though I was married and divorced twice. I'd had kids with my wife and knew then that it was a lie. I'd faked being in love, and I'd faked being married. I did love those two kids, though.

*I could share my money with them!*

I opened my mouth to suggest it, but what came out was, "I wish I was in love." My mouth was working on its own again.

They both turned to me, sympathy etched on their faces.

"Oh, don't look at me like that. I've tried being married...it's not for me." I sat on the armchair and gestured at the bed for them to sit. "I love myself, warts and all, and that's better than some guy could do for me."

Lucia shook her head, "You could have both, and you should have both. You're funny and smart, and you have strength—"

I waved my hand to hush her. "I'd be happy with respect from my family. And a diamond ring. Is that too much to ask for?"

"You shouldn't tell the universe you want to be alone. What if someone wonderful is just around the corner?"

"Tried it, didn't like it. I was married as a "straight man" and as "a gay man"—both ended up nightmares. Besides, I'm too old for that nonsense."

"That's unfair. You're a strong woman, Vee. Have the courage to change. To open yourself up to more." Jaqi looked so intent, it almost felt like an order, which brought up my Scottish stubborn like nobody's business.

"How about the courage to stay true to yourself?"

We just stared at each other, drunk enough to want to argue, sober enough to know better. I needed to change the subject, and it was a good opening to discuss what was bothering me about the money.

"What's unfair is me getting millions and everyone else only a few grand."

"I can't believe you said only. That money would build a deck and a second ensuite." Lucia pulled a bottle of red wine out of her overnight case and squinted at it. "Oh, poop. I thought it was a screw-up. Do you have a cork-puller?"

I shook my head and reached for the phone to call the front desk. They were happy to supply a corkscrew and said that I had a package at the desk, too. I told them that Jaqi would get them for me, her being the soberest, and I described her.

Jaqi headed downstairs, no doubt by the stairs rather than waiting for the elevator. Her fitness routine was based on impatience, but it worked for her.

"What are you going to do with all the money?" Lucia asked. I shrugged; I had no idea, until now my pensions had been enough. But now I had a house and a car. And a literal fortune.

"I think that you should take a trip. Go somewhere you always dreamed of, like the pyramids or the Grand Canyon." She hiccupped politely and grinned. "Or to Scotland, to see your ancestor's tombs."

That just reminded me that I had no idea where Aunt Bee was buried.

I leaned back against the fake leather.

"It wouldn't be the same alone. And I'm done looking for romance. Maybe I'll give half the money to my kids. Or Karey. She could use it."

"No! She would give it to her sons, and they don't deserve it. They would not appreciate it."

I had to agree, though I did feel a bit bad about Karey.

The door opened and Jaqi walked in, a corkscrew dangling from her fingers and a small box in the palm of her hand.

"It was left by the lawyer, Snapper."

"Snafu," I corrected her, holding my hand out for the box.

I fought with the tape wound around and around the little box. Honestly, it was like there was a monster locked behind ten walls in that thing. Did he have stock in the tape company?

Lucia filled Jaqi in on my thoughts about Karey, and Jaqi shook her head.

"Luci's right. They wouldn't appreciate it; they'd just say you were showing off your money. That way they could continue to resent you instead of having to admit you're a decent person."

"I know, but I feel so bad for Karey, and we seem to be getting along better this visit."

Lucia shook her head, dark eyes flashing. "You want too much for people to like you; the vampires can smell it. Especially those related to you, and they will use you and throw you away because their affection is not real."

I sighed and took the still unopened bottle from Lucia and handed the box to Jaqi. Soon I had the cork out and was looking in the bathroom for glasses, while Jaqi pulled a tiny switchblade from her pocket and cut through the many layers of tape.

There was only one glass and I'd used it to brush my teeth. Minty red wine, I don't think so. I handed the bottle to Jaqi and opened the tiny box. From the corner of my eye, I saw Jaqi take a pull straight from the bottle and hand it to Lucia, who did the same. Was I too squeamish about germs to drink? Nah, the alcohol would kill them.

I looked in the box.

The bottle was held out to me, but I was staring at the antique ruby and sapphire ring in filigreed gold that was nestled into some fluff from a pill bottle. It still smelled acrid, like aspirin.

It was Aunt Bee's favorite ring; she'd inherited it from her grandmother when she'd passed. It was originally my great-grandmother's wedding ring, and now it was mine.

And it was better than any diamond.

Lucia traded me the bottle for the ring box and gasped in delight. "This is from Mr. Snipper? He has a crush on you." She added in a singsong voice.

I snorted, "Even I'm not lonely enough to date him." But that reminded me of what I'd seen him up to with the secretary. "He's a creep. A handsy, molesting creep."

THE NEXT MORNING WAS a rare perfect, spring day for Ontario. There was a slight breeze, smelling faintly of lilac and early apple blossoms. The sun was bright and warm, and set in a lovely Simpsons sky. Like the TV show, small, very puffy clouds scattered around, none of them blocking the sun.

The walk was fairly short, only half a dozen blocks, but I was a bit chilled by the time we got to Mr. Sneakers office. I paused to look at the convenience store to the right of the elevator. It was crowded and a bit worn looking, like a gas station on a country road. Certainly not what I'd expect in a building with lawyer's offices.

I must've said that out loud, as the brown skinned man sweeping the cracked linoleum floor glared at me.

*Bee would have said, 'Well, shut my mouth", admonishing herself to think before speaking. She just loves the old southern charm.'*

Loved. Past tense.

I was hit with a wave of sadness and missed her so strongly, I could almost smell her perfume. Lucia must've felt it because she turned back to hug me. I didn't like the way the sweeper was eying us, so I just patted her arm and moved to the elevator.

Jaqi had already poked the button, but just like yesterday, it was slow as molasses. In February. In Iqaluit. Eventually it binged and the doors ground open. We stepped in, pushed the button and waited for the door to close. And waited. Finally, after Lucia had stabbed at it several more times, the door began to close, giving me plenty of time to smile cheerfully and wave at the cleaner.

I was surprised to find the lawyer's office dark and apparently closed. The glass panes beside the door showed no light at all. I looked at my watch, and it was almost nine-thirty. Granted, it was later than my appointment, but he and his secretary should be here. They were expecting me at nine. Did they give up and leave?

I stepped up and knocked on the door. It swung open a little on a creaky hinge. Lucia grasped my hand in hers, whether to stop me from going in or for comfort, I wasn't sure. And I've seen all those scary movies; I'm usually the one scoffing at the half-naked blond going into the haunted house just because the door opened. So, I really can't explain why I ignored the feeling of foreboding and Lucia's death grip on my hand, and pushed the door open wider.

"Mr. Scatter? Snapple?" I turned to Jaqi and hissed "What is his name?"

"Snapper. We should stay out and call the police." She waved a hand around in a small circular motion, as if it was sniffing the air coming through the open door. "Something is very wrong here."

But my hand pushed the door all the way open and I leaned in. "Mr. Snapper?" My voice came out a rough whisper and I cleared my throat. "Mr. Snapper? Are you back there?"

Silence, but a heavy one. A very speaking silence. It set the hairs on my arm rising up like a cat.

I gently pushed Lucia's hand from my arm and stepped in. The light switch was just where I expected it, a few inches from the door.

But the light didn't reveal the answer to where he was. Or where Miss Pineault was, either. Dammit, it's a workday, I had things to do. I strode boldly across the waiting room with the girls following me, and rapped sharply at his office door.

I suddenly remembered the scene I'd witnessed on Friday. Oh, my. What if they were at it again? I felt my ears burn, but I was more snarly than embarrassed. We had an appointment, so what if I was late.

Hoping to embarrass them both, I entered the room. It was empty.

"Oh," Jaqi peered around the corner of the door. "Where are they? Did they step out? We should look for a note."

Lucia slowly shook her head, dark hair falling unnoticed across her face. Silently, she pointed at the edge of Snack-cracker's desk.

It was spooky.It was creepy. As if I was being controlled by her pointing finger, I turned to stare at the corner of the dark, wooden desk. Nothing. The desk was spotless.

Then my eye was drawn to a spot of dark red on the sage colored carpet. My breath hitched as I recognized it.

Mr. Snipper's ox-blood red loafer. I remembered it from yesterday, it was so out of style. So tacky.

Like I was in a trance, I walked over to where I could see more. It was my lawyer, a knife sticking out from between his ribs, a pale blue suit stained with fresh blood. Fresh. It was still bright red.

Lucia pulled me to the door, but my eyes were fixed on that one shoe. His other foot was wearing only a white sock. Where was the other shoe? It seemed so odd and so sad to die without both shoes.

I think I was in shock. Nothing was making sense.

Someone was screaming. Then it got all spinny and drugged-looking.

I CAME TO, LYING ON the couch. I lifted the damp paper towel from my forehead and looked around me in confusion. Why was I lying down, and why did my throat hurt? Why did Lucia seem so pale?

It all rushed back, and I closed my eyes. I would never get the sight of him out of my mind. I could see it as I lay here, eyes closed.

"Vee? Are you awake?" Jaqi's voice was shaking. I'd never heard her like that before, so I opened my eyes and tried to sit up.

I made it, eventually. My heart hammered in my chest as my memory surfaced.

"Oh, my Lord, is he—"

"Dead. And your lawyer." Jaqi's rich brown skin was lighter than I'd ever seen it. Sweat beaded her hairline and she kept wiping her mouth.

She looked sick. I leapt up, all right, struggling to my feet, then I wrapped an arm around her shoulders. "Are you okay, sweetie?"

"I've never seen a dead man before. I just can't think past it. What do we do?"

I patted her arm with my other hand. It didn't help.

"Do you need to lie down? Or throw up?" I grimaced, that was such an indelicate phrase.

"No thanks, Vee. I already did." She looked guilty. "Right by the desk."

I frowned. I'd watched enough CSI to know that vomiting on the crime scene was a big no-no. "Did any of it hit Mr. ... er, the..." I couldn't say it.

She shook her head. Then she looked up at me, her eyes wide.

"We haven't called the cops yet. I was throwing up and then we were so worried about you," She paused. "How bad will that look?

I shook my head, "It doesn't matter how it looks. We have to call them." I checked my skirt pocket for my cellphone, but it wasn't there. It must have fallen out in the other room. I turned slightly to look in the office in case it was right there, but all I could see from this angle was one foot and the dark wood desk.

My ears started ringing, and I sank back onto the edge of the couch.

Jaqi eased down next to me and the three of us stared at each other.

Then my ears were pierced by the shrillest scream since Lady Macbeth saw her father-in-law.

It was Miss Pineault. She stepped out of the office, raised a shaky hand to point at me and screamed that I had killed him. I raised my hands to ward off the accusations, Jaqi stepped towards her and she fled the room, still shrieking.

Jaqi handed her phone to me and took off after her.

After a while, I heard sirens pulling up outside. By now all four of us were sitting in the waiting room, though Miss Pineault was as far from me as she could get. Jaqi was talking quickly into her phone; I think she was recording all the details for her next book. She looked way too calm to be talking to the police.

It seemed to take an hour for the elevator to arrive from the lobby, spilling the cops out into the hallway. My hands were shaking—I couldn't think past my lawyer being dead.

Just as I was about to struggle to my feet, Lucia placed a hand on my thigh. When our eyes met, hers sparked with worry. I kept my mouth shut.

The lead cop was big-boned, a blond with bald spots like a Siamese cat, right above his eyes. He was also rude, pushy, and generally unlikeable.

He started the investigation by practically yelling, "Who discovered the body?"

All four of us slowly raised our hands.

"All of you? Who found it first?" Lucia raised her hand higher as we lowered ours.

He stared at her silently as her hand lowered.

"And?"

"And what?" she whispered.

He sighed, like she was deliberately being obtuse. She shook my hand off of hers as I realized I'd been squeezing it. Why was it that half of the people I'd met here were so angry? Did somebody piss in the town's water system? You know, like in their cereal, but for the whole town.

Yeah, I was definitely in shock.

"And where is the body?" he growled at her, and my hackles went up.

"If you had asked that in the first place, you'd be done by now." I brushed off Jaqi's hand and stood, pushing my way to the angry officer. I saw the cute cop tense up, but I didn't care if he yelled at me. He was not treating an innocent girl like a serial killer on my watch.

"We had an appointment at nine this morning and arrived a little late. No-one was here, and when we peeked into his office, we... well, we saw his ox-blood loafer."

"Did I ask you?" He sneered and looked over my shoulder toward the cute cop, good cop to his bad cop, I guess. Or an actually good cop to his rude and incompetent cop. I crossed my arms and gave him my best *I'm not impressed* face—I've been told it was a really good one.

He just stared at me, then muttered to his partner, "Didn't I tell you? Almost twenty percent of hate crimes involve"—he gestured at me—"trans people."

"Yes, Sean, you did. And I'll remind you that the article actually said twenty percent of hate crime *victims* were trans. Not the killers, the victims."

"That's what's wrong with you, Shiomi. You believe everything you read."

I could see the muscles in Shiomi's jaw clench. I wondered what would happen if I gave him The Stare™ while telling him I wasn't trans. Not that I'm ashamed of who I am. I'd just love to see him swallow his tongue as he tripped over his words..

Shiomi asked where in the office I'd seen the shoe, and I said it was behind the desk. He nodded and gestured to his partner to go ahead of him. As he turned, I caught his sleeve.

"None of us actually touched the body. Once we moved closer, we could see the blood and his lower half, and that was enough for us. We came out here to call you."

He nodded and ducked through the door.

SHIOMI DIDN'T SHUT the door after himself, so I leaned in a little bit to watch. In a heartbeat, Jaqi was leaning in, too.

"Hey, Shiomi," I smiled at him as just another harmless female his mother's age. "Can we watch?" It sounded so macabre, but I wanted to see how they measured up to CSI.

"Miko," he responded. "My first name is Miko. And I suppose. As long as you touch nothing, not even the wall."

Miko had just turned to rejoin him when bad-cop grunted in triumph and held up a bloodied piece of clothing.

A pale lavender jacket. My jacket.

I screamed again in horror.

The secretary gasped and pointed a trembling hand at me. "That's hers!"

*How the hell did she get up in the door with us?*

I felt the blood simultaneously drain from my head and pound in my ears. I heard accusations fly at me as if they were spoken underwater. I heard later that I'd simply turned and sat on a chair, as delicate as a Russian princess. Then Lucia barged through and pushed my head down. Now I was in shock. And terrified.

"I didn't kill him," I whispered. "I still need my probate papers."

# Chapter Four

I sat on the little patio outside the hotel restaurant. I had my purse on the ground beside my chair and a coffee in my hands. The sun in my face felt wonderful and raised my spirits like nothing had happened this morning. A slight breeze off of the Rideau kept me from getting too warm.

We'd been questioned for about an hour, then had to give our names and addresses. As we talked, more cops arrived, these ones in hooded, white coveralls. They looked like earless rabbits. After that, we were told to go home.

I wore a pair of grape-colored capris and a white blouse with purple and pink roses on it, a silky pink scarf around my neck, and a pair of big sunglasses. I felt like Audrey Hepburn.

James came out and carefully set a plate of pancakes and eggs in front of me. With his other hand, he refilled my coffee and set down the carafe only long enough to pull more creamers from his apron pocket. He winked at me and turned to greet another customer.

I'll admit I had had my doubts about this place, but I was warming to it. They had the best staff I'd ever seen. So welcoming.

Not that every other place was unwelcoming. Ottawa was fine; they mostly ignored me like I was just any other older woman, or they went out of their way to be nice. Sometimes it felt like it was a bit forced, and some areas of town—*cough-Vanier-cough*—you just didn't go there.

But I lived in Orleans, a kind of bedroom community filled with senior care homes and co-ops, and I was happy there. It was more "none of my business" and "I don't care" than welcoming, but that was enough for me.

Though it was nice that the LGBT community here had welcomed me with open arms. They weren't that friendly in Ottawa, more of a pickup group and cliques. Of course, maybe I'd just lived there too long, and they'd seen too much of my shit to get excited to see me anymore. Like my drag-queen days, they were great fun, but really wild. You've seen nothing until you've seen a royalty of drag queens drunk off their heels in a biker bar.

That's what we called the gang of us. A royalty.

I remember the poor local bikers being confused about where to join in one fight. Should they side with the other bikers or with us, who went there after almost every show? We drank a lot and sometimes performed between the strippers acts for free, so they felt protective of us.

We didn't need them in the end. Oh, that sounded wrong. I smiled to myself.

We'd only had to smack down the leader of the French bikers before they all stomped out, yelling that the bar was a dive anyway.

Yeah, but it was our dive. I wondered where all the queens had ended up. I hadn't seen any of them since I'd quit performing nearly fifteen years ago.

I was jolted out of my reminiscing by a loud voice. Robert. Again.

It's a terrible thing to say, but I wish the doctors hadn't fought so hard for Karey to carry both the twins full term. Elliot might have been a good man without his brother.

In a strange turn of events, he didn't bully me right away. He even asked if he could join me for lunch. I didn't really want him to, I was enjoying my trip down memory lane, but I wasn't raised to be rude. And he was trying, right?

"Of course," I smiled as best I could. "Just let me catch James' eye to get more coffee for you."

He nodded and waited silently until the cup was placed before him. He nodded at me as he took his first sip. I wanted to believe that our relationship was about to turn a corner, but just couldn't. He was up to something.

It didn't take long to find out what as his father hopped the small wooden fence and joined us on the patio. He looked me up and down, then pasted on a smile.

"Hey, Fra... What was your name again?"

"Victoria. Long time, no see, Eddie. What's up with you these days?"

He laughed, staring at my breasts. "Things sure have changed, that's for sure."

I smiled weakly back. "I know, I was shocked to see The Kilt and Castle gone."

He paused for a second then laughed again. "How long you in town for, Vicky?"

Now that sounded like a friendly enough question, but Edward and I have never seen eye to eye. He's a football and hockey junkie, and I only watch BBC and the mystery channel. I also had a front row seat as he deserted my sister and returned only to bully her into submission.

So, he wasn't my favorite family member, and that's saying something.

"Just until the will is probated, probably. My life is in Ottawa, now."

"Well, your mom will be disappointed at not spending more time with you, I'm sure."

You'd think he'd never met any of us. In fact, it took an effort to not ask him that question. Instead I tried my best to be friendly and non-judgmental. I should have gotten an Oscar. Or at least an Emmy.

"I'm sure we'll see enough of each other before I go. And I have no idea how long it'll take now that the lawyer is dead."

He gave me a funny look before replying. Did he suspect me, too? I didn't really care about his opinion, except that he'd been family for over thirty years.

"So, what's exciting with you lately, Ed?" I leaned forward a little to show interest, but he leaned back in his chair.

"Not much, not much." He tilted his chair back at a dangerous angle and smiled at Debi, the cute little thing coming on shift. She smiled back and headed our way.

"Can I get you more coffee, Miss?"

"Oh, yes, please." It would be my third cup and likely would make me a bit jittery, but I needed the fortitude it would give me.

"Hey blondie, what have you got for a real man?" Ed grinned. I rolled my eyes.

The waitress winked at me, before saying,"I'll figure something out just as soon as one shows up, don't you worry. In the meantime, what can I get you two?"

I hid my grin behind my coffee cup. That girl would be fine.

Unfortunately, Robert saw my smile and scowled.

Next thing you know, a cop car pulled up beside the patio.

I didn't think they were that loud or that rude, but the cops were glaring at us as they got out of the car.

*Well, shit on a pretzel stick, it's Squinty and Miko.* And they were there to ask me more questions. Ed and Robert loved it, playing shocked and loudly proclaiming they had no idea I was a killer.

I'd call them assholes if I wasn't such a lady.

IT WAS A SMALL BOX of a room, empty but for a dented metal table bolted to the floor and an uncomfortable chair. They had taken my purse and my phone.

I decided to play it cool. Cooler than cool—I would be frigid. I tossed a look at the obvious camera hanging in a corner and tried to appear confident.

By the time the door opened, I felt bored. Bored-bored-bored. Garfield-hanging-on-a-screen-door bored.

I rolled my eyes as the stereotypical cop shuffled in and sat his donut-shop self in the chair opposite me. He set down a large gray box of files and pulled out a yellow pad and a pen. He glowered at me, trying to scare me, I guess, but he just looked like a pissed off Shih Tzu. Did I mention that I giggle when I'm nervous?

He hadn't even opened his mouth, and things already weren't going well. I thought I'd better explain what I knew before the interview got worse. How was I to know he wanted to ask the questions? This was the worst crime I'd ever "committed" until now. Well, the actual worst I'd been picked up for was getting drunk and fighting with another drunk, both of us too drunk to land a punch.

He wanted to know why I was there, why was the office closed in the middle of the day, why-why-why...

And one big how: How did my jacket get in the dead man's hands covered in his blood?

"Honestly? I have no idea. I mean, I realized after the reading yesterday that I'd left it there, but it should have been on the back of the pine chair, the one stained to look like mahogany. Isn't that tacky? The grains are completely different." As soon as the words left my mouth, I realized that tacky was the wrong word. His chest and my jacket were tacky—with his blood.

I felt myself pale and a buzzing started up in my ears. Suddenly, I couldn't get the sight of his feet out of my mind. One foot wearing only a sock, so pitifully unprepared for death.

Nobody should die wearing ugly shoes.

"What was that Mrs. Lilly?"

"Miss," I corrected him automatically. "I was just thinking that it's a pity to die in '80s ox-blood loafers, so ugly. What if he comes back as a ghost and has to wear those ugly shoes forever?"

"You think that's funny?"

"I think it's pathetic."

Our eyes met as he scowled at me.

"Why do you keep saying his bloody shoes? They haven't been tested for blood yet, is there something you'd like to get off your chest?"

We both glanced at my chest, it was small, but it was all mine. "I didn't say bloody, I said 'ox-blood.' It's a color. And something to tell you? Yes, I'm innocent, stop wasting time and look into his enemies."

"Any enemies in particular Miss Lilley?"

"He's a lawyer; he must have enemies. Nobody likes lawyers. Especially a boundary-impaired one. But I don't understand why someone would kill him. He is—was a creepy, handsy kind of man, but you don't kill over that, or there'd be almost no men left."

"So, you didn't like him."

"No, I didn't. But I didn't have to. He was a just a lawyer working on my Aunt Bee's estate. I wasn't in a relationship with him."

He scratched another note on his pad. "So, how would you define your non-relationship?"

"Business. That's all."

"But you didn't like him."

"Where are you going with this? I already said that I didn't."

He pulled out a bag from the box marked with what I assumed was the case file number. It was my jacket.

"So, if you weren't close how did he end up clutching your clothes?"

I remembered a court drama I'd watched with Jaqi last month. "Asked and answered. Move on."

He scowled again but did move on. "Alright, why did his secretary say that she saw you in an argument yesterday?"

I felt my mouth drop open.

"I did not argue with him, I..." How was I going to explain my own behavior? "I mean, He was getting too friendly, trying to, well, feel me up. So, I told him I was a trans woman and that he had better understand what he was getting into. Or something like that. It was just to get him to leave me alone and sign the paperwork."

"So, you did argue. How handsy was he? Were you afraid of him? Was it self-defense?"

"What? Don't be ridiculous, I'm a lady. And ladies don't—"

"Did he attack you? Attempted sexual assault? I'd understand if you panicked." He was clearly trying to give me a reason to confess, but he looked more like a kid lying about stealing cookies than a sympathetic ear.

"No, he did not attack me, nor did I attack him. He tried to fondle my thigh, and I removed his hand from my leg. End of the issue." I glared at him with my best Queen Elizabeth glare. Apparently, it needed work because he was not in the least bit intimidated.

"The secretary has made a statement that she came into the office after hearing raised voices to find Mr. Snapper leaning backwards over his desk, terrified, with you all up in his face." He stared at me, showing nothing. Neither anger, nor disbelief. He was a blank slate. Except for the twitch in his right eye.

"The secretary, who actually has a name, was mistaken. He wasn't terrified of me, and I never raised my voice. And I have never been *all up in his face* or anyone else's."

"The time of death estimate puts it about half an hour before your girlfriend called 9-1-1." He leaned closer to me and I forced myself not to react. "Right in the middle of your appointment. His secretary said you were due at nine."

"We were running late, we got there just before nine-thirty, and they were nowhere to be found." Besides, my knowledge of criminal investigations from TV told me that it was impossible to narrow it that precisely. It was usually within a couple of hours, like nine to eleven, although I didn't say that, of course. It would put us there within the window of opportunity.

He grunted as Miko opened the door and stepped in.

I felt my hands unclench under the table and my shoulders relax when Miko came in, even if he did have a tape recorder and another box of evidence. Surely, *he* would understand I was innocent.

As he met my eyes, he shook his head a bit. *No, what? No, we weren't friends, no he thought I was guilty? What?*

Miko set the box down hard, making me jump. He didn't even glance at me. I felt my lower lip quiver, and bit it to keep them from seeing. But the mean cop looked up and caught me. He grinned. It was not pretty.

I tossed my spiky, bangs and looked uninterested.

"So, we're recording this." He gestured toward the obvious camera in the corner and set a microphone in front of me that looked older than I was. "This is Officer Sean MacGuinty and Constable Miko Shiomi in attendance, State your name and address."

I cleared my throat and leaned toward the mic. "Victoria Rose Lilley, and I'm staying in that hotel behind the warehouses until probate is finished on my aunt's will. Econo-something."

"Did you kill her too? How much did you get in the old lady's will?"

I gasped, my heart seeming to miss a beat as tears jumped to my eyes. "I didn't kill either one. My aunt Bee was ninety-four and died in her sleep." I saw my hand was shaking as I brushed away a tear before it could drip down my cheek.

"Your lawyer was stabbed in the neck and chest. With a tiny, ladylike sword." He grinned again as I felt my face pale.

"There is nothing ladylike about that."

"Good thing you ain't a lady." That was enough to piss me off sufficiently that I was no longer feeling weak and scared. "I am a lady. You want to check my lacy panties? And that man was aunt Bee's probate lawyer, why would I kill him when he hadn't even finished the paperwork?"

"So, you were thinking of killing him for a while?"

"What? No!"

He held up my ruined jacket. I would never get the stains out.

"But this is yours?"

"Yes," I sighed; they knew it was. "I left it on my chair when I left the office yesterday after the reading. He probably picked it up to give back to me." I stared him right in his bloodshot eyes. "What possible motive could I have? I wasn't alone all morning. Are you even looking at anyone else?"

"I'll ask the questions. You've got a lot of lip for a suspect in a murder investigation. Talk much when you're nervous?"

"Not at all," I lied with a smile. "You don't frighten me; I know I'm innocent." He did worry me, though. He was just the type to put me away because it was easier than investigating.

"Got an answer for everything, don't you?" His lip practically curled as he pulled out a small, sword-shaped letter opener. I could see the blood was still wet by the amount it had left on the baggie.

Officer Shiomi leaned over to stare at the bag. "Hey, MacGuinty, why hasn't that been fingerprinted yet? It should've gone straight downstairs."

He reached for the bag, and the other cop pulled it away.

"Is that what you want? You want us to go by the book? Because once this is in evidence, your fingerprints will get you fifty years."

I smiled cheerfully, okay maybe a bit deranged, but if that was their only evidence...

"In fact, I insist on it! I never saw that thing before, and my fingerprints will prove it. Mr. Smacker was killed by someone else before I got there." I held my hands out dramatically.

They took me up on it.

I LOOKED AS ALOOF AND dignified as I could while they fingerprinted me and handed me a cheap tissue to wipe off the black ink. It tore, of course, but when I motioned for another they refused.

There was a wait to get me photographed against the height chart. Was there a line-up? How many innocent people did this useless git arrest today?

I was seated on a bench with a bunch of handcuffed folk. Most were sullen and silent, but this one pair kept whispering at each other. I didn't pay much attention until one mentioned the dead lawyer. I swear my ears perked up like a cat.

Did he say laundering money? Did he say illegal? Illegal what? I leaned toward them and whispered back.

"Are you talking about Mr. Snapper?"

They both shut right up and glared at me. Then Shiomi tapped my shoulder and it was time for my closeup.

Before I knew it, I was standing back in the lobby area where the girls were waiting for me.

"I am so glad to see you both, get me out of here," I whispered, my throat dry with nerves now that I was out. But they'd booked me. Fingerprinted me. It was a disaster. Suddenly panic gripped me.

I raced from the building, almost falling down the clean, white steps onto the postage stamp yard. I was shaking and crying. My heart pounding in my throat until I felt queasy. I stumbled to a parched looking tree and leaned on it, gulping air.

Lucia was alone when she caught up to where I was leaning against the mulberry tree and raised her big, frightened eyes to me. She was shivering slightly, so I handed her my sweater. She slipped it over her shoulders with mumbled thanks.

She looked shocky to my untrained eyes, and the dozen or so men standing about were staring at us like we were hardened criminals. They were absolutely no help.

"I think your lawyer's gone in to talk to the cops."

"My lawyer's dead, Luci."

"Not him, Jaqi got you a new one. For being a criminal."

For once I didn't find her English adorable, but I didn't have the energy to correct her. I sighed and tried to slide down the tree to sit on the grass. My skirt kept hitching up as the fabric snagged on the bark. I tried to stand up, and the darned tree tried to pull my skirt down!

Well, there I was, neither standing nor sitting, with my skirt stuck to the tree and sliding off of my hips. It's not like I have Lucia's hourglass figure. I'm more like a fitbit lean and sleek.

I was also stuck in a most uncomfortable position. Just then Shiomi, Jaqi, and a nice-looking black man stepped out of the police station.

I waved to catch Jaqi's attention, and Shiomi smiled when he saw me. If he was amused by my being stuck to a tree with my skirt half off, he was enough of a gentleman not to say it. But I was still pissed at him for ignoring me in the interrogation chamber.

"May I be of assistance, Miss Vee?" He was trying for a straight face, but a dimple was showing high on his cheek. If I hadn't been still angry, I'd want to kiss it, it was just so cute.

He untangled my skirt from a small branch I hadn't noticed and helped me over to his car. I sat in the front passenger seat, so I wouldn't look like I was under arrest. Again.

It would never do to set the town grapevine whispering if I had any intention of keeping the house.

That stopped me dead in my tracks, though I winced a bit at the turn of phrase. Was I going to stay in Aunt Bee's house? Did I want to live an hour from my best friends? It would make the winters lonely, that's too far to drive on icy roads.

But my heart rebelled at the thought of selling it. Bee had lived there for almost sixty years and left it to me as an act of love.

My eyes teared up again, so I missed seeing Jaqi and Lucia walk towards me. Their voices startled me when they spoke right at my elbow. The man with them must be my new lawyer. Thank the Gods.

"Are you alright, Vee?"

"Oh, I'm fine. Just tired and a bit horrified. And so confused."

"This is DeShane Wilson, he's the lawyer for criminals." Lucia nibbled at the edge of her nail.

I cringed at her turn of phrase, and DeShane stepped forward, holding his hand out to shake mine.

"I went to pre-law with Jaqi. She's explained the situation to me."

Before anyone could say anything else, a big white van with the local TV station's logo on the side pulled up. It was followed by a pale blue van with the national network's logo. The drivers jumped out, quick as can be, and started pointing cameras at us.

That was enough. I was not going to be front and center on the news.

I heaved myself up, overbalancing a bit in my hurry, and grabbed Lucia's arm to steady myself. As I saw the cameras start to circle, it occurred to me to seem too weak to be the killer.

The word tasted foul, killer. Murderer. I shuddered and Lucia wrapped her arm around my shoulder and led me to Jaqi's car.

I DECIDED TO GO TO Aunt Bee's bank as soon as I could. I had a buzzing itch in my brain that told me I was missing something, and I needed to move fast. Of course, it didn't tell me what I was missing, so, I decided that the bank was as good a place to start as any. And it should be easy, as Bee had changed the accounts to include me years ago.

I should at least get a copy of the last statements from her accounts and a look in the bank box.

Boy, was I wrong.

"I'm sorry, but I can't share client accounts to just anyone off the street."

I fought to stay smiling and calm. "I'm not just anyone, I'm her heir. And her lawyer told me that my name was on the accounts as a joint holder or whatever."

"I need to see your driver's license for that. And a copy of the probated will."

"I don't drive and the lawyer—"

Jaqi leaned in, "How about we discuss this with a manager?"

"Well, he's a little busy—"

"So are we. Get him out here." Jaqi was firm but polite, no doubt trying out a character for a future book. She sounded almost cop-like.

The teller tried to quell her with a stare, but you remember that bit about Jaqi sending the soldiers running? Yeah, that.

We sat on slightly uncomfortable chairs facing a balding, lean as a rail, youngish man. He looked nervous, sweat beading on his shiny pate, his face pale. Of course, as a natural blond, maybe that pale was his normal.

It turned out, after I offered to have my lawyer in to look at all of the bank's records of Bee's services for the probate, there was a way to see the security box, but not the bank records. He assured us that they would have been mailed out, so we should check the house. And we could only look at the box contents, not remove anything.

If I hadn't been so set on looking at the bank records, on doing something right now, I would have thought of checking the house. We followed the manager down a couple of hallways, then downstairs to a big, old-fashioned door. It had a lock-pad and once through, it was scrupulously clean and modern. Brass doors covered every wall from knee height to over my head. The air was on the cold side of fresh and raised goose bumps all over my arms.

He walked over to a post-office box looking door on the far side of the room. Inserting his key, he held his hand out to me.

*Oh, right, my key.* I reached into my purse for the ring of keys Slapper had given me, but I didn't find it. Feeling my face turning pink, I assured him that It was in my purse somewhere and pulled my bag up and onto a plain table square in the middle of the room.

But it wasn't in there. Where had it gone? I dug around some more and finally spilled the entire thing onto the table.

My keys were gone.

# Chapter Five

We assembled in my new lawyer's office at noon. I brought take-out for everyone because the only availability DeShane had was on his lunch break. We would need to be quick, too; he was due in court at one-thirty.

The priority need was to strategize my defense. My stomach dropped at the thought of going to court, of being found guilty because I'm different. Could we get a jury of twelve trans women? Or even gays, lesbians, and bi-folk?

The lawyer shook his head, a wry twist on his lips. I was speaking my thoughts out loud again. '*Shut my mouth!*' I could almost hear Aunt Bee's voice again.

DeShane started off the meeting with a big bite of curry, nodding at me. So, I said what was on my mind.

"We need to find the real killer. The police are focused on me because of my jacket. They aren't even looking at anyone else."

DeShane nodded but his mouth was too full to comment. Although he did try, making a muffled and incomprehensible merf-merf noise.

"Victoria, that's crazy talk." Lucia wasn't shy about her opinion, and as DeShane nodded emphatically, Luci waved her hand at him, dropping a bit of rice on his fancy leather blotter. Why do all lawyers' offices look like a gentlemans' club from the 1800s? I shook myself—solve one mystery at a time.

"Look, I know I'm innocent," I said, "So who really did it?" I leaned forward to spear a chunk of green curried chicken before Jaqi ate it all." There can't be too many people with access to the office."

Deshane swallowed. "You'd be surprised. Cleaners, delivery guys, mailman, other lawyers, his secretary."

"I don't think she has the stomach for it. She screamed like Jamie Lee Curtis when she saw the... him."

Lucia agreed. "There was a lot of blood. Even got some onto the wall."

DeShane waved his hand and swallowed. "Then there should have been blood on the killer. Did they test your hands for blood?"

I shook my head, relieved for a moment. "No, but they have my jacket, it was soaked in blood."

He grinned, white teeth flashing. It was the first real smile I'd seen in a while. "Soaked, not sprayed in a straight line?"

"No, the whole front was soaked, like I'd been sprayed by a fire hydrant. But isn't our blood under pressure? It might spray like that if he was scared."

DeShane was still grinning. "Not like that. Not even a little bit like that."

By the time he rushed back to court, DeShane had a written list of possible suspects and a couple of people who had seen us go into Shuttle's office. One person was on both lists; the cleaner downstairs.

Of course, there was no way to know motives at this point.

Luci and I were walking in front of Jaqi as we debated where to start. Who should we talk to first? I could feel Jaqi's disapproval on the back of my neck like a spider. I turned and sure enough, she was staring at me, a slight frown between her eyebrows.

"Do you have a better idea?" I asked.

"Yes, let Des handle it, he's trained for this. He has a pretty good record of acquittals, too."

"Pretty good isn't good enough. How long do you think I'd last in a men's prison?"

"You won't go to a men's prison, Vee."

"And just what are you basing that little nugget of wisdom on? The caring and understanding nature of the local cops?"

Her face flushed, and her lips pressed together. I knew I'd pushed it too far, but I felt trapped, panicked by DeShane saying to take the charges seriously. There was a brief moment when an apology for my tone would have stopped things from going south, but I said nothing.

As Jaqi stomped away, I yelled that apology, but it was too late. She kept walking with no sign that she'd heard me.

I swallowed around a lump in my throat. Why was I taking it out on Jaqi? I hated fighting with my friends. I felt so stupid and alone.

"She will be fine; she's just worried about you."

"I know, gods, I'm such a jerk sometimes."

It was just a skip and a jump to the office building where Mr. Snapper had died. I didn't like the word murder. It was so graphic. We hid in a recessed door across the street to see who came in and out.

It was so boring. Why does it look fun on cop shows? After what seemed like hours, my feet were hurting in my tasteful pumps, and I was getting a backache from standing still so long.

I needed a cup of tea, STAT.

I glanced around for a cafe, knowing full well that there wasn't one in sight of the shop. But he had coffee and tea. I knew he did. I'd seen it when we here the first time. It hadn't looked very promising, but beggars can't be choosers.

We entered the store by the lobby door, glancing at the elevator in passing. That reminded me: I still didn't have a new probate lawyer.

DeShane was supposed to be looking into it, but he was in court all afternoon and busy with my defense. Maybe Miss Pineault would know. We'd go up after talking to the shopkeeper.

We walked confidently through the glass doors and headed for the coffee island. There was one of those huge brown carafes marked Hazel-Van, which must stand for hazelnut-vanilla, and it sounded so good.

"Look at this, Luci; doesn't that just make your mouth water?"

She read the label and smiled, "Ooh, let's get that. It will make me up for being so dull."

I knew she was distracted by my fight with her lover, but it was worse that I'd imagined. She was clearly thinking in Spanish and translating to English. She only did that when she was really upset.

"Oh, honey, why don't you go make sure Jaqi's alright? I can handle this."

She smiled up at me, "Are sure? You will be lonely."

"I won't be lonely; there are lots of people here. And I think I'll stop by the Bun Journee for a treat before coming back to the hotel." I wanted her to know that she had time to, well make it up to Jaqi for coming with me, rather than going with Jaqi.

She grinned widely and took off toward the street door. Message received.

I poured myself a cup of the flavored coffee, and it did smell lovely. I added just enough cream to make it change color and one packet of artificial sweetener. After all, if I was going to eat at Ben's, I'd better cut back on other things. A girl needs to watch her figure, after all.

I held back, waiting until the last customer left, so I'd have a bit of time to ask questions. Before I could move, he appeared at my elbow and glared at me under lowered brows.

"Why are you standing here? You have to pay for coffee, even the ones you drink here."

I smiled back. "I was just thinking how good this coffee is. I didn't expect..."

"You did not expect good coffee from a dirty store?"

His brows lowered even further. I had commented on how run-down the place looked the first time I was here. But I'd said it out in the lobby. This man must have ears like a hawk, hearing a mouse rustle from two hundred feet in the air.

"I'm so sorry I said that. I was in such a state, I didn't mean it. My favorite aunt had just died, and I was here for her will. I was just so upset." A tear thickened my voice at the mention of Aunt Bee.

His expression changed immediately, and patting me on the shoulder, he led me to the counter and pulled out a box of tissues. Now, I don't normally use tissues because they make my nose red. They are made from wood fiber, you know. But I wanted him to talk to me, and the damsel in distress thing seemed to be working.

He looked around the store, avoiding my gaze. Probably to give me time to pull myself together, but I was going to milk this for all it was worth.

"It doesn't matter," he said softly. "You were right, but it is not my doing, the owner is too cheap to pay to fix things. There is a hole in the floor under the soda machine; mice get in from the basement. Does he fix it? No, he gives me a bag of poison. Cheap."

I nodded. Maybe Mr. Snipple had been harassing the building owner? Maybe he threatened him?

So, of course, I asked who the owner was, and that theory was blown away. Sniffer had been the owner.

"And now what am I to do? I cannot fix things even with my own money now. He is dead, and who do I pay my rent to? Who do I complain to about the floor? He paid me to clean the whole building, who will pay me now? What if it is months before things are settled? What do I do if they say to close the store?"

I nodded in agreement. He certainly sounded angry with Snapdappler, but angry enough to kill?

"I am in neverland. Never get fixed, never look good. And the people upstairs, they are young. What do they do now?"

"What young people?" I hadn't seen anyone but Snapple and Miss Pineault in the building.

"They are on the third floor, a group of students. They come here from another country to study in Ottawa. If the building is closed, where do they go?"

I shook my head; I didn't know they were here, much less where they could go now.

Maybe I should talk to them. They might be able to find a place closer to Ottawa if they look now. Students are leaving for the summer soon."

He smiled and waved away my money when I offered it to him for the coffee.

"You a nice woman not like that vain one upstairs. She is so much better than us, she looks at me like we are rodents. He gave me a hoity-toity look to show me what he meant.

"You mean Miss Pineault?"

He nodded vigorously.

"She was here, early that morning. Looking around like she was queen of the city. The face she gave me when she saw me watching." He laughed, "Like I am scared of a little girl like her."

I smiled with him, making this a bonding moment. After all, I had more questions.

What time had Miss Pineault arrived? Because she said she'd arrived after us, didn't she? And these students, who are they, where did they come from, did Miko know about them? What about other clients? If he was handsy with all the women, where were their husbands that morning?

Mr. Patel waved his hands in the air to make me stop talking.

"I answer one more question. I am busy man."

I paused to collect my thoughts. "Do you know of anyone who wanted Mr. Snapper dead?"

To my surprise, he nodded.

"There was a man, a week ago, he was yelling at Mr. Snapper on the street."

"Why? What did he say?"

"That he would kill him, is that not what you asked? He was angry for Mr. Snapper abusing his wife. She is a teacher, very sweet. Always so polite to me."

"Abusing her? What did he do?"

"I do not know, but the man punched Mr. Snapper in the belly. Made him puke everywhere, which I had to clean up." He frowned again.

I needed to make notes of who was where, when and why.

I needed to go visit Benoit.

I WAS REGRETTING HAVING decided to walk up the two flights of stairs instead of taking the elevator. As I wheezed on the landing outside the door to the upstairs hall, I fully understood how Jaqi kept so slim. Those stairs were hard work.

Finally, I tugged the door open.

The hallway was filled with a smooth, almost jazzy, music. It smelled green and dark, with a touch of skunk-butt. I could also smell a sweet curry, maybe nuts and apples. Maybe coconut.

Suddenly, I was starving.

I'd ask a few questions, then get a snack. The door was answered after a bit of scuffling noise and a suspicious silence.

A young man opened the door only far enough to see him. He blocked my view of the apartment with his body. But he had dark eyes and thick black hair, his skin was even and tan, and he looked like he smiled a lot. Plain but attractive enough.

Of course, now that I was here, I had no idea what to say.

"May I help you?" He was so polite and had a faint English accent. I held out my hand and introduced myself.

"I am Fadi," he said in return. "How may I help you?"

"Well..." *How does one ask a stranger if he's a murderer?* "I was here the other day when Mr. Snapper was attacked. I was wondering if you saw or heard anything unusual? I'm just..."

I wasn't sure how to finish that sentence. Fortunately, Fadi stepped in to fill the silence.

"Of course, it must be very frightening to a woman of your age. But we are accustomed to things like this in my country. I was not surprised to hear that the man was killed. These things happen to wealthy men."

"It doesn't happen here very often—very rarely, in fact. It must be scary where you're from." I tried to smile, but I probably just looked unbalanced since it occurred to me that he acted way too complacent about a murder. Complacent like he had nothing to worry about, as if the killer wasn't gunning for him and he knew it.

Which could mean...

I shifted my weight as if my feet hurt, which wasn't really a lie, and tried to see past him. He moved with me, still blocking my view. I smiled again.

"Are you boys okay living here? Aren't you worried the killer might come back?"

He shook his head, his hair falling over one eye before he flicked it away.

"No, we fight for ourselves. We have no worry. Besides, we saw nothing. We were here or in class. We never go to the second floor but to pay our rents."

Huh. Snap-on was killed in the middle of the month, so the boy did have a point.

"So, you haven't been there for a couple of weeks, then. I really hoped you'd have an idea who hurt him, so I'd know I was safe. What if someone killed Mr. Snapper because I was seeing him that morning?"

I hadn't really thought I was in any danger, so why did my voice quaver? It really helped sell it though; I did have to admit that.

After glancing over his shoulder, Fadi opened the door to let me in and offered me a cup of tea. I thought that sounded delightful until I heard him tell a roommate to make this old woman a tea because she was feeling weak. But I swallowed it, figuring this newly-bestowed *old bat status* would probably make them better about answering questions. But it did stick in my craw something fierce.

The tea was wonderful. They made it in a pot on the stove, boiling the water with honey before adding the loose leaves. I saw the package, but it wasn't in English. Too bad, it was lovely.

And the ritual of serving tea did calm their fear of what I might represent.

I lost count of the number of men living there, the whole place was just a kitchen, a living room and bedrooms. Based on the number of students living here, the whole third floor must be bedrooms.

"How much do you pay to live here, if you don't mind my asking?" I knew it wasn't my business, but my spider sense was tingling. This arrangement had to be illegal.

"We pay one thousand each for our rooms. We buy our groceries together and share our food. Like back home."

"A thousand a month *each*?!" I practically screeched.

"Yes, it is a good deal, no?"

"No," I assured him. "You could get a two- or three-bedroom apartment for a thousand dollars a month."

He glanced at his roommates as they all stared at me, then I assume he repeated what I said in his own language, since they all started to look angry.

Then Fadi turned back to me, his eyes black. "Then this dead man is a criminal?"

I nodded, at least in this way, and I was afraid in a lot more ways. The guys at the jail had mentioned money laundering.

I asked a few more questions, but the only real news I got, other than their exorbitant rent, was that Fadi's younger brother was staying at the college with a friend. At least, Fadi thought so. He hadn't heard from him in days.

And didn't Fadi look worried when he said it.

I left soon after giving them my cell number, in case they needed anything, and accepted an invitation to dinner when everything was settled.

They seemed to be nice young men, but that didn't mean anything. They were way too calm about the murder and too angry about the rent. What if they were only pretending that this was the first they'd heard of it?

I WAS TURNING INTO Aunt Bee. The orange-spiced, black tea, the almond croissant, the lazy flirting with Ben. If I had to turn into someone other than me, she was the best possible person to be.

I smiled as Ben came to sit with me, a nutty-smelling coffee in his hand.

"How are you today, Mademoiselle?" His hair was tucked into a tidy hair net with the poochy bit that holds it together in the middle of his forehead.

I itched to move it to the back where it would hide in his black hair.

He grinned at me and straightened it to the exact center of his forehead. What a brat.

I laughed though; it was so obviously done to bug me.

"Bee hated me wearing it like this too. She said I looked like a gang-banger from a cheap 90's movie."

"So, of course, you stopped immediately." I raised my eyebrow. He bellowed laughter, shaking his head.

I had just joined in, still itching to fix it, when my phoned rang with bright Latin music.

Before I could even say hello, Lucia was talking fast.

"The police are looking for you, they were just here. I had to tell them where you were, they said you were running to avoid arrest. I didn't know what else to do. Oh, Vee, what is going on?"

My mouth dropped open, and then firmed into a thin line. That jerk cop had terrified Lucia. I could hear it in her voice.

"Calm down, sweetie. What did they say?"

"They said you were a killer and that running away would just make things worser on you. They said to arrest us for hiding you. They said they would send me back. They didn't mean Ottawa, Vee. I can't go back to Columbia." A deep breath sounded down the phone line, and I knew that she was trying to pull herself together.

"It's okay Luci, they can't do anything because I didn't do it. And I talked to the cleaner guy and have a whole new list of suspects."

"Oh. Good. I know you are innocent like a baby, but that fat policeman is mean like a snake. Do not trust him."

"Oh, I don't. He would love to pin this on me. But I think Miko's a good cop."

"The best cop." Ben whispered. I nodded and repeated, "The best cop, so don't get yourself into a panic."

I had barely hung up when Miko and Himself came in. Speak of the devil and he shall appear. Squinty MacGuinty trod heavily onto the tile floor, making as much noise as possible. He grinned when he saw me.

I calmly took another sip of my tea, tapping my lips with a napkin. Miko nodded hello but allowed his partner to take the lead.

They stood next to us, forcing me to tilt my head into an uncomfortable position to stare them in the eye. Aunt Bee could look down her nose while looking up at the second floor, so that's what I did. Ben raised a single eyebrow at Miko, then turned his head to Squinty.

"Is there something I can get for you, officer? A coffee to go?"

"It's detective, and you mind your own business, or I'll haul you in for aiding and abetting." He scowled at Ben, like a bulldog.

Miko motioned for Ben to stay seated when he would've stood up to argue.

I turned to Miko, my voice as steady as I could make it. "Is there a problem Officer?" I took a lazy sip of my now cold tea.

"Detective," MacGuinty glared even more ferociously at me, but I didn't rise to the bait. I figured that if I could keep him off his game, he might make a mistake big enough to get the charges dropped.

"You are under arrest for the murder of David Snapper. Stand up and put your hands behind your head."

My mouth dropped.

"Are you serious? Did you even look at other suspects?"

He smiled, showing his teeth.

"There are no other suspects. I found the killer right here."

My heart dropped. He wasn't even investigating. And I didn't have anything new to tell him.

Except for the students. And my missing bank keys.

He hauled me to my feet by one arm and jerked it practically out of its socket when he twisted it behind me to put on the cuffs. I needed my phone call; I needed my lawyer and Luci to come help. But when I asked for my cell phone lying on the table, the jerk pocketed it.

"Ben, call my friends. They're at my room at the hotel."

Ben nodded as MacGuinty shoved me toward the cafe door.

# Chapter Six

Again with the dull, gray walls and the scarred table. Again with the Keystone Kop routine. I waited, trying to look relaxed.

When the door opened, I was surprised to see neither Shiomi nor MacGuinty. It was a fresh-faced young woman I'd never seen before. She started and looked confused when she saw me.

I faked cheeriness. "Who were you looking for, dear?"

She blinked and adjusted her uniform collar. Then peered at the door number and looked puzzled.

"I was looking for Detective MacGuinty. He was supposed to be in here with a suspect."

I grimaced, feeling my lips draw back.

"Squinty's in here with me. Well, he was. I think he's in his office or the break room. He's trying to break me, you see."

I smiled, widening my eyes to look innocent and a bit batty. She wiped a grin from her face at my nickname for the detective. I guess she didn't like him either. Color me shocked.

"Sorry, Ma'am, I must have it wrong. He said he had a suspect."

I sighed, weary of his macho, bull-headed, anti-trans bullshit. Before I could explain, Squinty came barging back in shoving the uniformed woman out of his way.

"What do you think you're doing, Smith? Interfering with a murder suspect? Just because your great-grandfather was one of the founders—"

Smith straightened her shoulders and gazed straight into his bulging eyes. Her chin may have quivered a bit, but her voice was firm as she gently set him in his place.

"A report just came in that involves your suspect. There's a 10-62 at 115 Watson Lane."

"That's my house." My throat caught, roughening my voice. What was going on? Squinty glared at me but I didn't care, someone broke into Bee's house.

MacGuinty finally looked at Officer Smith. "Anyone on scene?"

She nodded, "Two officers on-scene, but the intruder is—" She glanced at me.

Squinty glared at me and dragged Smith out into the hall, slamming the door after him.

Now I worried that it might be Karey and Robert again. Or Robert and Eddie, or maybe Elliot. Oh hell, I was sure it was Robert. And there was nothing I could do, a neighbor must have called 9-1-1. It was out of my hands.

This would destroy Karey and any chance of making up with my mother. She would never believe it wasn't my fault. I could strangle the little shit.

AFTER A MINUTE OR TWO, MacGuinty came back, red in the face and somehow worried at the same time.

"How did you do it?"

"How did I do what?"

The lines of his face creased like fissures in rock.

"How did you arrange to have that dump broken into? It won't work; you're still my top suspect."

I didn't know whether to laugh or scream, so I did neither. I got really calm.

"Offic-Detective MacGuinty, I didn't break into my own house. I've been here for the past hour and you have my phone, so how could I arrange anything? And why would I, it's my house! Anything I want, I can just go get. My keys were stolen, probably by my nephew Robert at breakfast."

He scowled again—did that man have no other expression?

"Why didn't you report them missing before now? Eh?"

I laughed in his face; I just could not help it. "When would I have done that? While you were dislocating my shoulder at the cafe? While you were ignoring me in here? 'Oh, by the way, if my house is broken into later, I just want you to know my keys are missing.' Not suspicious at all."

He sat down and looked me in the eye. He seemed to be recalculating my innocence. I hoped so, anyway.

"When did you get the keys and when did you notice them missing?"

"Day before yesterday, Snapper gave them to me after the reading. I noticed they were missing when I went to the bank today to introduce myself as Bee's heir." Was he rethinking my guilt, please God?

No. God never did listen to me.

"You could have handed them off yesterday. Easy enough to arrange then."

"And how did I know I'd have you as an alibi?"

"You would have had Shiomi's husband. Almost as good." He grinned.

I was surprised to hear no derision in his voice when he mentioned Ben; husband just tripped off his tongue like it was nothing. Was all this racism and homo-trans-phobia just an act? The man might be smarter than I thought.

That didn't make me feel better at all.

# Chapter Seven

I was still in the deadly dull interview room, but MacGuinty had sent for a cup of tea and a sandwich for me. Neither was as good as Ben's, but I was starving. I guess worrying eats up a lot of calories.

Shiomi was at my house overseeing the investigation, since it was probably linked to Mr. Snapper's death.

I'd gone to town on a yellow legal pad, jotting down my suspect list and clues. I had a lot of the former and almost none of the latter. MacGuinty still seemed doubtful, but at least he listened.

I went over who had had access to the office, who definitely had a beef with Snapster, and who might have had one, such as the husbands or sons of women he'd been grabby with. I repeated what Fadi and the shopkeeper-slash-cleaner had said.

I wrote it down for Squinty with arrows linking names and motives. Timing and alibis I didn't know, since his estimated of time of death had been so obviously made up.

I should not have said that out loud. His face darkened.

I hurried to mention that Miss Pineault was a bad suspect because of her screaming when we found the body, and the shop-keeper-cleaner had been too busy with the morning coffee rush, though he did have a good motive. He was being used by the lawyer-owner.

I didn't know how to find out about husbands or sons, or if asking whether their wife or mother had been molested or not by their lawyer seemed a little too bold. It would piss them off if they hadn't been, and piss them off worse if they had been, if that made any sense.

MacGuinty nodded. I relaxed back into my chair.

"Or you could have done it for your aunt's estate, and this is all a smoke-screen."

*Hell's bells!* He was a better actor than I thought, but was he acting before or acting now? It hurt to think about.

"I already inherited everything from my aunt. Didn't you read the will? That should have been your first move."

"You know your aunt's file was stolen, so there's only your word you were even mentioned. Your nephews tell a far different story. They were the major heirs and you're stealing their rightful inheritance." He grinned in triumph.

I just sat there, shocked. Why did they lie? Did mom support their lie? Did Karey? Why was the will missing? Okay, that last one was obvious, and it pointed straight at my flame-trousered nephews.

No wonder I was the chief suspect.

It was near dinnertime when they finally released me with more warnings to stay in town. That reminded me that I needed to find a new probate lawyer. Or maybe there was an agreement with another lawyer to take over.

The Castor Bean trees were in full bloom and the vanilla scent was heavenly. The sun shone from a perfect bowl of robin's egg blue. Such a lovely day to spend dealing with jerks.

I walked along with my eyes on my feet, worried about what could go wrong now.

Before I knew it, I was back at Bee's, standing on the lawn with the girls. They wouldn't let me in, they were still fingerprinting. I wasn't allowed to go to supper either, as they would need me to tell them what's missing as soon as they were done.

I dug Benoit's card out of my purse. It was time to see if he had a delivery service. He said he could send the food by taxi, with me paying for both the fare and the food. I agreed and turned back to watching cops in bunny-suits troop in and out of the cheery cottage. The butter yellow paint with royal blue trim always reminded me of the French countryside.

It looked way too pretty for the cops hanging about the yard.

I needed to ask Miss Pineault about a new probate lawyer. Did Mr. Snapper work with other lawyers? Or did I need to find my own? I searched for the letter in my purse. It had had their phone number on it but it wasn't in there. I must have left it in the room.

A few of the neighbors had gathered across the street and the young female officer was questioning them. Smith—that was her name.

I waved at her and she smiled back. I knew I shouldn't interrupt in case one of them saw the break-in, but *what if* one of them saw the break-in?

So, I scurried over, trying to look harmless and cheerful instead of determined and upset. Luci says I can be a bit scary. Hah, in *this* dress?

They peered at me curiously, except for one old guy who grinned with teeth too big and perfect to be real. He reached out to shake my hand, so I let him.

"You don't remember me, do ya, girl?" He turned to the others, waving his hand at me, "This is Bee's niece, you remember her."

A few nodded, most looked uncertain. He was still holding my hand.

"I can't say how sorry I was to hear of Bee's passing. She was a wonderful woman." He wiped his eyes with his other hand. "Such a handsome woman, and so smart. You look just like her, ya know."

I smiled and gently disentangled my hand. "Were you close to Aunt Bee?"

He chortled, "Closer than she wanted some days. I was a bit sweet on her; don't know she returned the feeling. Always kept to herself."

"I'm sure she was fond of you, she talked about a Burt next door."

He grinned widely. "That's me! Bless her heart."

Smith pulled me gently aside to remind me that she was investigating the break-in, and I shouldn't be talking to potential witnesses.

But Burt interrupted her, and the others agreed that it was better to have me there because I was family.

They were all eager to give me their condolences and share memories of Bee with me. I teared up; they were so sweet. But I could see Smith getting antsy, so I steered the conversation back to the house. If they knew who did this, it would be a race to punish them. Me and Smith, toe to toe.

I'd kill whoever did this to Aunt Bee.

They didn't know much. They'd recognized Robert and Karey the other day, so none of them called the police. Today, Burt heard a noise like breaking glass from inside while he was watering Bee's flowers. He peered in but nobody was in the front room, so he went home to dial 9-1-1.

We had a definite time, them. And since the thieves were gone when the cops showed up, they must have run as soon as they heard the sirens.

Smith nodded as she took down Burt's contact information. As she walked back to the house, I invited everyone to Bee's for a wake after I had a chance to clean up. Two of the women, Greta and Helen, were widowed sisters living up-street, and offered to help with setting the house to rights. Bee would have liked that.

I heard a car door slam and pulled out my wallet as I turned to get the food. It wasn't a taxi, it was Ben. He held a large paper bag and looked seriously worried.

"What are you doing here? Who's running the shop?"

"Good to see you too, Vee." He frowned, his lips turned in a bit, as if he was fighting chewing on them.

"I'm sorry, I don't mean to be rude. I'm hungry and worried sick."

He reached out one arm to hug me, and then handed the food to Jaqi to deal with.

"Vee, Miko is worried about you. He says that you're asking questions and doing your own investigation."

"Well, you knew that. And if I don't nobody else will. His partner has already had me fingerprinted to check for other crimes. He's bound and determined to see me arrested."

"But Vee, what if you already questioned the killer? What if he thinks you know it's him?"

"Then they will make a mistake."

"Or try to kill you. They've already killed once."

I hadn't thought of that. Maybe I should warn Fadi. Find out what his brother said when he got back.

I looked at Ben and he gazed back, little worry lines circling his amazing blue eyes.

"You're right," I whispered hoarsely, fear gripping my throat. "It hadn't occurred to me. But no-one else is looking to clear my name. My family lied about the will, and that makes me a solid suspect."

"I thought Lucia and Jaqi alibied you."

"They did, but MacGuinty thinks they're the ones lying. He threatened to have Lucia deported."

Ben's jaw firmed and his eyes seemed to darken. I reached out and laid my hand on his shoulder. "I have to keep looking, I can't go to prison."

"No," he agreed. "You're far too beautiful." As I shook my head, he cast his eyes over my shoulder to glare at the cops.

I WAITED SOMEWHAT PATIENTLY at the bar. I would have preferred to be at the hotel where the staff knew me, but Miss Pineault—Seline—had insisted this one was more convenient for her.

I glanced around at the suits and pencil skirts and figured that it was more her style than the Samurai Cowboy, whether it was convenient or not.

At least my simple summer dress fit in well. It was fifties inspired, mint green with a white collar and white sandals. The white belt gave me an illusion of a waist, and I'd worn a cheery flowered scarf around my neck.

My trim figure had garnered me a few looks from the suits. I could see them stealing glances in the mirror behind the bar.

It did wonders for my ego, which had been suffering a bit lately.

I used the time to call Fadi to ask about his brother. He was still missing and now they were getting scared with their landlord dead and Farouj gone. It looked bad. It took a bit of work, but I convinced him that the best thing was to report him missing and get the authorities involved.

"The murder was about my aunt Bee somehow. They'll know Farouj had nothing to do with it. Maybe they'll be able to ask questions you can't."

"You are very wise, Miss Victoria. I already asked his friends and his professor, but I do not know his fellow students. Maybe the police will know."

I hated to think it, but could Farouj have seen something on his way to class? His disappearance the same morning was suspicious. It could also mean he was the killer. Would Snapple have trusted him to get that close? Of course, he would. If he was paying his rent.

SELINE WAS LATE, WITHOUT an apology. Her red power suit put my dress to shame, and clashed with it. But I was here to get information, not a date.

I waved at the bartender, and she came over with a refill of my tea, dropped off lunch menus, and raised an eyebrow at Seline.

"I'll have a large glass of Pinot Noir." She turned to me with a quizzical frown.

"So, why did you call me? Are we friends now?" A cold smile tugged at her lips.

"Well, I don't see why we should be enemies. And I did have a few questions."

"Of course you do," she said as the rich, red wine arrived in front of her. I noticed that she said nothing to the bartender, not even offering a nod. You can tell a lot about a person by the way they treat staff.

I didn't like her. But I smiled anyway.

"I was wondering what becomes of my aunt's estate now. Without a lawyer and the will missing..." I smiled brightly, hoping she'd think I was naïve, so she'd say more than she meant to.

"Why do you think I know?"

I raised my eyebrow back at her. "But you worked for an estate lawyer. You must have learned a lot from him. I could tell right away how smart you are."

She grinned, agreeing with my flattery.

"Of course. I learned all I could, I wasn't going to be a secretary forever, you know. I'm going to law school in the evenings."

I clapped my hands in delight, thrilled she was so willing to brag. Now, how to get her to blab about the killing? Did she have any clue what really happened?

"That must be terribly hard, the law is so confusing."

She smiled, "It's simple so far. Just estates and torts, and what a lawyer is allowed to do with a client."

"Allowed to do?" I leaned in, wishing I could blush on command. "You mean like sex?"

She laughed, its sound loud in the hushed atmosphere. Several turned to look at us. "You are certainly not supposed to do anything like that." She smothered another laugh. "But if some old bat wants to leave you something for *services rendered*, that's no big deal."

I nodded, was that why he was so handsy? Of course, it was. Ew. "I suppose he was very popular with women of a certain age. He was very charming." The lie tasted foul, but it worked.

"He was very smart and very charming when he wanted to be." She waved for another glass, so I took a sip of my cooling tea. "But you want to know about your inheritance. I don't blame you; it was a lot of money." She took a big swallow from her glass. "It must be driving you crazy to be so close to it and have no way to get it."

I nodded, gritting my teeth. "Yes, but also the keys that Mr. Snapper gave me are missing, so I can't open her bank deposit box. Or get to the antiques inside the house." I watched her face carefully. "Especially as it's a crime scene now."

Her eyes widened slightly. She hadn't known.

"I was at the office the other day looking for you, and I ran into this boy who lives upstairs." Whoa, I better slow down. My wine glass was nearly empty; I didn't remember drinking it that fast. "He said he was renting a room on the top floor. Did you know about that?"

She rolled her eyes. "Yes, I knew. I already said that I do the bookkeeping. I made a spreadsheet to track who paid and who I needed to remind."

So, she knew about the probably illegal apartment up there. I still needed more, though. In her position, she would see a lot of paperwork and a lot of people coming and going. Did she know Fadi's brother was missing?

I glanced at her to see how drunk she was. My eyes focused on a lovely, antique pin on her lapel. It was made of silver filigree, with pearls and sapphires. So familiar. I reached out my right hand to touch it and she automatically brushed my hand away, staring at me before relaxing.

"What a lovely piece, and so familiar." I stared at it; something tickled the edge of my brain.

"I was wearing it the day you... found David."

"Of course." I 'd been so distracted, it was a wonder I remembered the pin at all.

I was halfway back to the hotel when I realized Seline had never answered my question about knowing the missing boy. But at least I knew that everything was in the air about the will until it was found, or my family stopped lying. I could ask Des about how we could handle that legally.

I pulled out my cell and called his office. He could see me tomorrow. He, too, had news.

BACK IN OUR ROOM, I caught the girls up with my Seline interview and my appointment tomorrow. We were making a list of questions I still needed answered. Like a to-do list. *Oh, I'd better add a to-do list.*

Where was Fadi's brother and why was he missing?

Who broke into the house, though? I was certain that Eddie and Robert had done it. They could easily have swiped my keys at breakfast while I was distracted by the cops.

I'd helped Miko make a list of the damage. The roll-top desk was wrecked, and all the bank papers gone. So were a few small antiques. And things like sugar and flour poured all over the kitchen. Her bedroom was also tossed, and my heart ached at the thought of a thief going through her private things. If I ever found out who did it, I'd break their fingers. Well, I'd threaten to. Maybe Burt would do it for me.

Why was I being framed? And by whom? Though I could be pretty certain it was Eddie and Robert again.

The biggest question was who killed Snapper and why? I underlined that.

The girls had no more answers than I did. So, who did we question next? I felt I'd gotten as much out of Fadi and Seline as I could, and both were still suspects. What if Fadi killed Snapper and his own brother? Over what? I underlined that three times.

And Mr. Patel, shop manager-slash-cleaner still had a great motive. Did the man he'd told me about even exist? How would I find him?

Next, I had to find a lawyer willing to take over probate in this mess. Of course, since the lawyer drew fees from the estate, it would be a juicy contract. Maybe I'd play that up.

And I'd talk to the shop-keep again, he might know more about that morning. He didn't like Seline either. Did he enjoy a good gossip?

We'd sent out for pizza, so when there was a knock at the door, Jaqi opened it without first checking who it was. It was not pizza.

Squinty was dangling handcuffs from his middle finger. Bad things also come in threes. I was going to miss dinner again.

At least I was losing weight.

# Chapter Eight

I waited, yet again, trying to look relaxed—yet again. After what seemed like an hour, I put my head on the table and fell asleep. If they were trying to worry me into a state, they hadn't counted on my insomnia these past few days.

I awoke with a start when the door banged open and Squinty MacGuinty barreled in. He looked smug, and that was a bad sign. He flung an old folder onto the desk. I could see Frank Vincent Lilley on a white label across the top of the file.

My heart sank. Shit, I should have expected him to find that.

He smirked at my expression.

"Mr. Frank Vincent Lilley. I've got some interesting documents here."

"I went to court to legally change my name. Besides, you're not my mother; you don't get to use my middle name."

"Trying to hide from your criminal past, eh?"

"Oh, please. It was all minor stuff. Teenage stupidity. It's hardly the record of a hardened criminal."

"You were a teenager at..." He made a show of looking at the pages in the file. "Thirty?"

"There were no charges that time. A neighbor called the cops on me arguing with my wife. I had already left by the time they got to the house."

"Your wife made a formal complaint and asked about a restraining order."

"But she changed her mind, and all charges were dropped. The real last charge was when I was twenty-three. Almost forty years ago. Forty. Years. Ago. I don't think it'll stand up as a pattern of criminal behavior."

I would have to thank Jaqi; I wouldn't have thought that her constant bouncing ideas off of me would become this useful.

He glowered and started reading all of the charges out loud, noisily ruffling the paper as he did. If it was an intimidation technique, it failed. I knew what was there, and how useless it was to him.

When it became clear I wasn't scared of the records coming to light, he changed tactics. He pulled out my next most recent mugshot and slid it across the table. I was an effeminate boy, large, green eyes and dirty blond hair. It was too long for my thin face and made me look like a scruffy mongrel. It didn't help that I was drunk and had a stupid smirk on my face.

But I just shrugged and pushed the photo back to him. He didn't like and grabbed the photo, holding it at arm's length in front of my face.

"So, you think it's fine if I leaked this shot to the press? This one and your newest mugshot, side by side, with a history of your criminal records?"

I paled a bit. It wasn't that nobody knew, it was just so hurtfulrude to deadname someone. So inappropriate, so devastating. But I wasn't about to let him know that. I smiled.

"Do whatever you think best."

He smirked and left the room.

Shit. Was he really going to leak that photo? I wasn't ashamed of who I was or the road I took to get here. And my arrest record? Pfft. It was all drunk and disorderly stuff. Anger at myself back in the day because I didn't like myself. Many young people go through that, though probably not on the same level. Still, drunk and arguing, drunk and smashing my own stuff, drunk and fighting...

Of course, this didn't mean I wanted it to be public knowledge. *Hello, can't a girl get some privacy?*

Plus, Aunt Bee's neighbors probably had no idea. They were old-fashioned and would not be thrilled. Also, I was planning to live there.

What was taking so long? Was he on the other side of the mirror, watching me slowly break? Or was he calling every newspaper he knew in the region? What if he really was releasing it? I sure as hell didn't want it out there. It wouldn't be safe to have it out; trans women were still being murdered for just existing. The last thing I wanted was to be another cold statistic.

Not to mention my mother's reaction. *I mean it, let's not mention my mother.*

How long was he going to take? Maybe he went out for dinner, maybe I was forgotten here with nobody daring to release me without his say-so, and he's gone home for the night. I groaned. I hate waiting. I also had to pee.

I waved at the unblinking red light in the corner. Nothing. I waved a bit more frantically but after waiting a few minutes there was still no response.

I was getting desperate.

I crept to the door and was surprised to find it unlocked. Of course, it occurred to me that this was a test, that I'd be arrested if I left, but things were beyond desperate. I was hopping like a five-year-old. It was all I could do to keep my hands from physically holding the pee in.

I took a deep breath, peered both ways down the hall, and slipped out. As I recalled, the bathrooms were almost back to the lobby. I set off at a trot.

After much relief, I returned to the interview room to find chaos had broken out in my absence. Squinty MacGuinty was hollering orders and questions without pause for breath. Younger cops milled around looking ashamed and lost.

After a few minutes, one spotted me and tapped MacGuinty on the shoulder. Bad move.

"What the hell do you want? Think you've found the prisoner cowering behind me?"

"Um, yessir. But she's not exactly..."

"What?" The shout nearly blew the rookie's hair off of his head. If Squinty was that angry, my best move was to be calm and compliant. Or was that my bitchiest move. Either way, I smiled brightly when the youngster pointed at me, and MacGuinty spun around.

I waved and smiled sweetly. "Were you looking for me? I just had to step out for a tinkle."

He turned white, then blood surged into his face so fast, I actually worried about him having a stroke. Would that be considered killing him?

I cautiously moved back to the door to the room, passing right under his arm as he leaned against the wall. He smelled of sour sweat. *Oh dear, had I really gone too far?* But there was no help for it; I really had had to use the toilet.

Looking into his angry face, with his brows clenched so hard there was a white outline around his eyes, I softened. Yes, he was a jerk and a transphobe, but he was still a person. The same thing I was demanding that he see me as. I deflated.

"Sorry, I just really needed to pee. I'm back now."

Oddly, MacGuinty wasn't pleased by my return. I thought he'd be glad not to have lost an interviewee, but who can tell with men. *Am I right?*

He sat down hard, making the table shake, going for heavy intimidation. But I had come to a sort of moral decision in the bathroom. I was going to help the police because this guy was useless at solving such a terrible crime.

I smiled gently, "Is the recorder back on? I'd like there to be a record of this."

He growled but turned it back on, stated our names and the date and time. All very official.

Before he could say anything else, I leaned into the mic.

"Since the fingerprints will prove me innocent, I think we should discuss other suspects."

"What the—"

But I just cut him off and kept talking. Holding up my pinkie, I started listing facts and suspects.

"First off, the manager of the store on the ground floor is a very angry man. He practically bit my head off for asking him a question. Then he told me he was in an ongoing disagreement with the victim over repairs and maintenance and was losing customers because of it. Second, did you know that the top floor of the building is an illegal apartment with who knows how many foreign students in it? I was so shocked when I found out. And the amount he's charging them should be a crime. Oh, I suppose it already is."

His expression softened. He was actually listening. I smiled at him and held up finger number three, no wait, bad finger! I held up my index finger but that just looked odd, so I lowered my hand to the table.

"Third, the letter opener probably came from his desk, so it was someone who had access and that he would let that close."

He pointed at me.

"No, other than me. Someone like his secretary or another client. With his creepy flirting, I probably wasn't the only person angry with him. In fact, I'm sure I wasn't."

"So, you admit you were angry with him? Did you argue? Fight?"

I sagged as my optimism fled; he still thought I did it. At least it was being taped.

After he'd turned everything, I was trying to tell him around on me, I asked for my lawyer. I should've done it hours ago, but he was likely to still be in court. Or in bed by now. What time was it? I asked for my phone to call DeShane.

I also asked for a piece of paper and a pen. I got the paper, but Squinty handed me a crayon. Said he didn't want me committing suicide on his watch. With a pen? How creative does he think I am?

While waiting for my girls, or my lawyer to show. I wrote out my columns: suspect, motive, opportunity, clues.

The shopkeeper: He'd been fighting with Snapper for years. Maybe he snapped. *Snapped on Snapper? Cute.* He was also cleaning the building for less than minimum wage as part of his lease agreement. He saw when people came in or out; he could know when Miss Pineault had gone out.

Miss Pineault: They were having an affair, and he was hitting on me, probably others too. She could have killed him before going out for coffee. Of course, the affair wasn't likely to have been serious, and how would such a tiny thing have driven that letter opener into his chest?

The students: I didn't know much about them aside from them being young, male, and foreign. I knew that they paid a lot more for college than Canadians did, and were being cheated on the rent. Were they running out of money? And why had Fadi kept telling me to ask his brother, who was missing since that morning?

I had no clue about his other clients. If he only did estates, then he likely had a lot of older women. If he threw himself at them the way he did to me, maybe one conked him with her purse? Or her husband stabbed him?

There was a lot of unexplored area here.

He left me alone again, but I felt calm this time. I didn't feel like the jaws of prison were open wide to gobble me.

He'd taken the pad of paper, but I still had my blue crayon. I drew a Venn diagram on the table, Snapper in the middle and my suspects in overlapping circles with their motives and opportunity.

Who could have done it? There were too many suspects. How to narrow it? I was sure that Karey was innocent but the men in her life...not so much.

I was pretty sure that Seline was innocent, she was too vain to risk getting her designer shoes bloody. And why would she have done it? What was the motive? After our meeting last night, I was pretty sure she didn't do it. And definitely not out of jealousy.

What was the cleaner's name again? Now, he had reason to be angry, what with being screwed on his lease and cleaning contract. Having to buy his own cleaning stuff probably cost more than he was getting paid, and he had no way out of the contract without losing his shop lease. Had I explained that to Squinty?

I would leave him a note when I left, assuming I could leave.

I was running out of room for more notes when Des walked in.

He stared at the table before shaking his head and smiling.

"Going for an insanity defense?"

Anyone else and I would have been snarked, but I could see those perfect teeth shining despite his being silhouetted against the light.

"Can you take a photo of it for me? They took my phone from me again."

# Chapter Nine

It was nearly sunset when they finally released me with more warnings to stay in town. The deep pinks and faint traces of purple were lovely but failed to raise my spirits. This whole week had been a nightmare.

I walked along with my eyes on the sky, worried about what else could go wrong. And whether Squinty actually gave the press my records. Was that even allowed?

I was so preoccupied that I nearly ran into a woman struggling with her dog. I glanced up and was surprised to recognize Seline.

"Miss Pineault, what a pleasure to bump into you. Almost literally." I grinned but she just glanced up from her dog and scowled.

"Oh, do you need help with the leash?" I offered.

The dog tried to scoot over to me but was tangled around her ankles and nearly tripped her. I quickly picked up the—chihuahua? I think. Maybe a bit of corgi? It was a gold color in spots and had a curly tail. And it was bald as my uncle Elmo. Poor thing.

"Let go of my dog," she barked, "I'm in a hurry."

Now most folk, even when they're impatient, get a certain tone in their voice when talking to or about their pets. Not Seline; she sounded furious. Quiet but furious. Scary actually.

I gently set the dog down, and it immediately tried to jump on me again. She kicked it, yelling at it to sit. I was shocked. Who the fuck kicks a little dog?

But, still smiling, I tried to be reasonable. At least long enough to get the poor baby away from her. From the way it was cringing at her feet, this was not the first time she'd done this. I watched her carefully pull one foot from the tangle of leash.

I couldn't help but notice her fire-engine red pumps, so gorgeous. Louboutins, or a really good knock off. As she raised her second foot to get free, the dog whimpered and stared me right in the eyes. My heart broke for the poor, scared thing.

"Do you need a hand with her? I don't mind. I love dogs." I smiled, trying for reassuring. I must have looked comforting because she scowled and handed me the leash.

"If you could keep him for a few hours, I'll be ready to get him before nine. Where would you be?"

"By nine, I'll be at my room in the hotel by the discount store. It's room 341."

She sighed as if it was a major effort to walk the few blocks from here to the Econotel, but I smiled back.

She patted her outfit back into place, and I noticed she was wearing the same pin on her lapel, a circle of filigreed silver with pearls and a sapphire. A nagging itch at the back of my brain said I was missing something.

"I can't get over that lovely broach. Is it antique?"

She glared at me as she covered the pin with her hand and stalked off. I looked down at the dog.

Poor wee mite, he was shivering as I picked him up. He stuck his nose under my chin and squirmed right in, his little tail wagging.

He looked so pathetic with his shivering, his missing fur, and overall timidity. I might have just fallen in love. Would that satisfy Lucia's romantic heart? Probably not.

LUCIA WAS A MOTHER hen by nature, and the dog got her full-on, overprotective, mama-bear attention as soon as I walked through the door.

She squeed like a ten-year-old at an ice cream party with extra sprinkle colors.

While Jaqi shook her head, Luci picked up the nameless dog and buried her face in its unfurry belly.

"Who's the cutest widdle puppy? Who's got a smoochy widdle face?"

I cleared my throat. "Um, Luci? That's a full-grown dog. A chihuahua, I'm almost pretty sure. Maybe." I peered at the tiny pooch tucked under my bestie's chin. "It would be easier to tell if it had any fur."

Lucia glared at me and covered the dog's ears.

"He thinks he's a handsome boy. Don't you go telling him he's ugly."

"I didn't. I said he was bald and I'm pretty sure it's not news to him."

She scowled at me. Jaqi wiped her grin away and tried to look serious.

"Where did you get him? What were you thinking, buying a dog? You know I'm allergic."

I opened my mouth to explain but Luci scurried over to Jaqi's side, holding the dog up to her face. As Jaqi backed away, covering her mouth and nose to avoid breathing in any... um, fur, Lucia exclaimed over how sweet and well behaved he was. And that no fur probably meant no allergies.

Jaqi glared at me.

"I didn't buy a dog. This is not our dog, I swear." Luci turned to me. "Whose dog is he?"

I sat on the edge of the bed. "He belongs to Seline, I'm just keeping him while she runs some errands."

"The Miss Pineault who accused you of murder?"

I shrugged. "That's not the dog's fault."

"It is her! Why would do her any favors?"

"It wasn't a favor for her, she was mistreating Baldie here."

Lucia's face grew serious and a little scary. Her dark eyes almost glowed with anger. "Mistreated, how?"

I squirmed a little. Even Baldie seemed to watching me, to hear what I'd say next.

"She was yanking at his leash and yelling. She might have kicked him. A little."

Her brows lowered, and I felt glad I rarely saw her truly angry.

"Okay, she kicked him," I said. "That's why I offered to take him. I couldn't stand the thought of this little guy getting kicked again."

Somehow, Luci managed to soften her expression while her eyes remained hot and furious.

"She will not get this sweet boy back again to kick."

Jaqi leaned forward, "Honey, that's stealing, and Vee's already in enough trouble because of that woman."

"Then she will give him to us. That isn't stealing."

"And just how are you going to work this miracle?" I should have saved my breath. Luci just handed the ugly thing to me and went into the bathroom.

Jaqi yelled after her, "We can't keep a dog, I'm allergic."

Lucia hollered back, "Vee just inherited a house. Plenty of room for such a small thing."

The dog looked up at me with huge, expressive black eyes and whined. He was shaking with nerves. Very gently, quivering the whole time, he placed a paw on my wrist and wiggled up to lick under my chin.

I sighed. I knew when I was beaten.

"I think I'll call him Victor."

It was well after ten by the time Seline showed up. Her rap at the door had me bolting from where Victor and I had been dozing. My heart thundered almost painfully in my chest.

WAS IT THE COPS AGAIN? Would Squinty manage to charge me this time and make it stick?

He'd warned me to keep out of the investigation several times. Would he think I was just muddying the water?

Luci glanced at me before pulling the door open. She blocked my view, but I could tell that she disliked whoever was on the other side of the door by the set of her shoulders and the way she tugged her T-shirt straight.

"Can I help you?" Her voice was steady, but she sounded as if she didn't know the other person. Odd.

But it was definitely Seline's voice.

"Miss Lilley has my dog."

"I don't know this—"

Seline shoved Lucia out of her way and pointed at us in the chair. Victor started shaking again. He was terrified of this woman. How could I keep him? My mind spun but found no solution other than reporting her, and then he'd go to a pound, not me.

While I was thinking, Seline had stepped into the room, glaring at me. Luci moved to stand between us, leaving the door open.

"I know what you've done."

Seline blanched at Luci's words. Or was it the murder in Luci's eyes?

"I don't know what you're talking about." Seline licked her lips. Her voice was haughty, but she looked nervous.

I held Victor on my lap and he leaned into me. Seline moved to look at me again.

"Just give me my dog, Victoria. Come on, Charley." But Victor-Charley just whined.

A mean look passed over Seline's face so quick, I might have imagined it. Except for the tiny dog shivering, whining, and trying to disappear into my armpit.

"I know you don't love Charley," I tried to sound calm and reasonable even as something about her gave me the willies. "I saw you kick him, and he's terrified of you. Why not let Lucia have him?

Seline crooked her finger at Victor. "I keep what's mine. Chardonnay, I'll count to three."

Chardonnay? Seriously? But he stood up and minced his way to the edge of my chair. He glanced at me, and then jumped down, going to this awful woman.

"Seline, I just don't understand. Why do want him back when you clearly don't like him? We're willing to take him off your hands."

"Because he's mine. My dog, my collar, my property."

Lucia pulled Seline's arm, dragging her attention back to her. "Victor is a living being, not property. You can have his collar and leash, but I am keeping the precious boy."

Seline shoved her again, and Luci tripped in the crowded room, hitting her head on the wall. Jaqi sprang off of the bed, her braids whipping with the speed of her movement.

She shoved Seline up against the door frame, holding her arm just short of choking her.

Seline was practically spitting, she was so angry. "You will be sorry you touched me. You will all be sorry."

She grabbed the dog and stalked off. The back of my neck was cold. There was something in her voice. Something... evil.

Luci and Jaqi shared a look, then Jaqi shook her head. "Leave it alone. We don't need her calling the police on us. Think of how that would look." She gestured at me, and the anger fell from Luci's face.

"I am sorry, Vee. I wasn't thinking."

I nodded, "That's okay, sweetie. I'll call around tomorrow to see if there's anything to be done.

# Chapter Ten

I should have known it would be a horrible day when I awoke to pounding rain. It was after eight and still so dark that no light showed around the curtains.

Jaqi and Luci must have gone for breakfast already, as their bed was mussed but empty. The bathroom door was open with the light on.

I grunted as I pushed myself up. Time to wash up and go smell the coffee.

They weren't in the restaurant either, but despite my cute pink sweater set, I was cold, so I decided not to head to Bun Journee. If they got worried, they'd call.

James was on duty again. Did that man never go home?

I waved at him and pantomimed drinking a coffee. He grinned as he turned to reach for a white mug.

I wondered if I'd ever eat here once I moved into Bee's house. I watched as a teenager carried a stack of newspapers to the bar. He fiddled with the top one while waiting for James to pay him. Then he turned and as his eyes met mine, he stiffened and leaned over to whisper at James.

This wasn't a normal reaction; this was something else. My temples tightened as a headache prompted by the weather and sudden anxiety flared behind my eyes.

James brought a paper when he came over with my coffee. He looked serious, a small frown marring his forehead.

"Vee, you might want to head back to Ottawa for a few days." He glanced around at the mostly empty restaurant. "Or at least stay in your room.

"What... why?" I stammered. Was I no longer welcome? Was this Seline's revenge, telling everyone I was a thief?

He slid the paper across the table, and I almost fainted from shock. MacGuinty had done it. He'd really, actually done it.

Splashed across the top of the paper were my last mugshot and a photo of me now. The headline screamed: "Is There a Killer Loose in Town?" I turned away, the coffee sitting like acid in my stomach. I wanted to crawl under the table and might have done it if James hadn't touched my shoulder with his warm, steadying hand.

"I'm so sorry, Miss Vee. I can arrange for your meals to be delivered to your room, if you'd like.

I stared at his soft, brown eyes. Then around the room, seeing one or two people jerk their eyes back to their plates.

"No," My voice was barely above a whisper, "No, I have nothing to hide, I didn't do anything."

AFTER SUFFERING THE stares and whispers for another fifteen minutes, I signaled to James that I was done. He nodded and brought me my bill and a coffee to-go. I signed the bill and hurried upstairs, tears stinging my eyes.

I wanted to run back to Ottawa so badly, my chest hurt.

How had this happened? How had things gone so wrong in just a few days?

I LAY DOWN WITH MY arm over my eyes, trying to relax. It wasn't working; I kept seeing those mugshots.

What would Burt and the sisters think?

*Oh, my lord, what would my mother think?*

I didn't have to wait long to find out. My phone rang, and I knew it was her. Even the ringtone sounded shrill.

Drawing a deep breath, I answered it. I tried to sound cheerful, but Mother cut right in.

"So, you've seen it. What were you thinking?"

"I thought he was bluffing. I thought it was illegal to release those photos."

"He? He who?" her voice was clipped and tight. I could just picture the way her lips pressed when she was truly angry,

I sighed and got more comfortable on the bed. *This might take a while.*

"Squin—Detective MacGuinty. He's determined to pin everything on me: the break-in, the murder, the missing will."

That reminded me. Mother had sided with the boys and claimed I wasn't inheriting very much. "And may I say thank you for throwing me under the bus with the cops? Lying about Aunt Bee's will just made me suspect number one in her death, too."

"Don't be ridiculous, Bee was ninety-four. She died of old age."

"Well, tell that to MacGuinty when you go to take back your lies."

There was a brief silence, and I winced, waiting for her anger to hit me like tropical monsoon.

Instead her voice was quiet. "Sean MacGuinty was such an unhappy child. I'm not surprised he grew into a bully. His father was a drunk, you remember."

She took his side.

For an instant, I couldn't breathe. My mother had sided with the man trying to put me in prison.

I was as surprised as she must have been when my mouth opened and spoke in a gentle voice: "Thank you for all your love and support, Mom. It means the world to me to have you in my corner."

Then I hung up the phone.

As I picked up my pillow to suffocate myself, the phone rang again. Without even checking who it was, I sent it to voicemail.

DID YOU KNOW THAT YOU can't actually suffocate yourself? Your body won't let you; you need another person to push the pillow into your face when your body pushes it away. Oh, don't worry. I knew that from reading Jaqi's books, not from personal experience.

I'd just held the pillow to stifle my scream. I knew I was way too fabulous to deprive the world of my glory, or at least that's what I'd tell myself. But truthfully, I was too danged stubborn to kill myself. I'd rather make others suffer watching me be happy and well, fabulous.

I stayed on the bed for a while. I wondered where Jaqi and Lucia were. And why they didn't call when I never showed up at Ben's.

As if thinking about them called them to me, my cell blared Latin music. I debated sending it to voicemail but answered it instead. I wasn't angry with them, so it was unfair to take it out on them.

"Vee, where have you been?" Lucia's voice was loud and happy. I hated to ruin her mood.

"Have you seen this morning's paper?"

"No, Ben doesn't have the newspapers here. He says it ruins your digestion."

"Well, one of you better go get one and call me back."

I hated being so abrupt with her, but I couldn't trust myself to explain. I hung up and waited.

Ten minutes later, a Native drumbeat vibrated my cell to life on the bedside table. Jaqi.

IT WAS ONLY THREE O'CLOCK, and it was already one of the longest days of my life. I dressed down in a pair of jeans and a Smiths Falls T-shirt. No make-up, my hair left loose. It was short enough that I might be mistaken for an effeminate yet grungy man. Punk and New Wave, together at last.

Although I desperately wanted to cancel my shopping trip with Karey, I knew how much it meant to her. I just didn't want to be recognized.

We met at a small park near the Rideau Canal. It had been a bit of a walk, but that gave me time to clear my head. I tried to get back to the confident, I-don't-care-what-you-think attitude of yesterday, but I did care about this.

I was devastated and furious. I wanted to hide and to kill that man. But by the time I got there, the sun had worked its magic, and I felt much more at ease.

Karey was waiting near a memorial to the town's founder. It was in the open area and easy to spot. I raised my hand to call out to her but noticed her shoulders were hunched forward and her head bowed. She looked miserable. She must have had a terrible time when Eddie and the boys saw the paper.

Despair washed over me like a heavy blanket. Maybe Mom was right about me. I just brought trouble wherever I went.

I walked over to Karey and laid a hand on her shoulder. She started, then smiled weakly. I sat beside her in the hard-stone bench ,and we stared at the statue of a fat, smug, white man.

"I'm sorry. I didn't know that was going to be in the paper."

She nodded, "Mom was absolutely livid. I've never seen her so angry."

"Yeah, she called me."

There was an uneasy silence for a few minutes.

"Do you still want to go shopping?"

"Not really, but if you want to, I'll go." We sounded like strangers and my heart broke a little more. There couldn't be much left of it.

"I'd rather head to Murphy's Irish and get plastered."

I laughed in surprise. "That doesn't sound like my prim and proper baby sister. The one Mom brags about all the time."

"Screw mom, let's go get a drink."

# Chapter Eleven

Murphy's Irish Pub was near the locks on the canal. Not the pretty touristy side, the one where the workers lived a hundred years ago. Dark and dingy, it suited our moods perfectly.

We got a couple of stares coming in, but nobody looked long enough to have recognized me.

We sat for a while waiting for service, then Karey sighed and stood up. "What do want, Vee? I think it's all beers and hard stuff."

I smiled up at her, "See if they have Guinness. It's an Irish pub, after all. If not, maybe they have the Perth beer. It's local enough."

They did have Guinness, and I sighed in pleasure as the bitter, chocolaty goodness hit my tongue.

Karey had picked something red and light. It looked good, but my "beer that eats like a meal" was better.

A couple of hours later, and I'd forgotten all about the newspaper. Well, mostly. Karey and I had claimed a booth near the bathrooms. At my age and me drinking beer, bathrooms were important.

The booth apparently got table service, and we'd drunk more than we should have. I ordered a plate of fries, figuring that even a pub couldn't screw that up.

I was wrong, they were mushy. But they did soak up a bit of the booze so we could keep drinking.

That's where Eddie found us when he dropped by his favorite watering hole. Apparently, this was *his* bar, and we were both encroaching and embarrassing.

Not an issue, mostly because I didn't give a rat's woohoo if Eddie was embarrassed.

His face flushed, and I realized I was speaking out loud. "Oops, didn't mean for you to hear that."

He scowled. "Are you leaving or what? This is my bar."

"I didn't know you bought a bar." I hiccupped in a genteel fashion and peered up at him, impressed.

He growled. It was equal parts scary and sexy. Okay, even I knew I was drunk, now.

"Karey, we should call a cab."

She glared at Eddie, "No. Why should we? We were here first, if he doesn't like it, he can go elsewhere."

At least, I think that's what she said, she was slurring more than a bit.

Eddie leaned in and whispered. "You are going home to straighten out. How dare you embarrass me in front of the guys?"

"Well, they had no idea who we were until you started making a scene." I thought I was being quite reasonable. But Eddie's face darkened.

He turned to the bar, "Sam, get these ladies a cab. They're done here."

Aw, he called me a lady.

We took a cab back to the hotel and decided to get some real food in our bellies. I was expecting to be charged with Snapper's murder at any moment, so I wanted something good to eat.

James took one look at us and hurried over. He seated us in a quiet corner and brought coffee while we looked at the menus.

He was so sweet. We ordered cheeseburgers and more fries, and then obediently drank our coffee. I didn't want to disappoint James.

I did feel better after my belly was full, though Karey still looked a little green.

"Why are they doing this to you?"

I shook my head, then swayed as I realized how bad an idea that was.

"I don't know. The lead detective is stupid and hates me."

She frowned. "Does he even know you?"

He was about twenty years younger than me, so I doubted it. "I don't know. Maybe he did it and is framing me." Suddenly my heart pounded, and my head cleared.

Did he do it? Could he have done it? It would explain a lot.

But nobody had mentioned him, and cops do stand out. I should go back and ask Patel and Seline, maybe Fadi. But I remembered he wasn't there, Farouj was still missing and he was searching for him. Had he found his brother?

I motioned to James for more coffee. I was about to pull an all-nighter.

Karey sobered up about an hour later and started pulling my notes towards herself as I wrote feverishly on napkin after napkin.

No one could have done the murder; at least, not if I believed their alibis. So, who was lying?

So, I laid it all out for Karey. She nodded and gasped in all the right places. Seline was a monster for abusing Victor-Charley, but at 5'5" and 120lbs soaking wet, could she have driven a letter-opener through a man's chest?

The cleaner was strong and angry enough, but he stood to lose too much by Snapper's death.

The students were a mystery; I still didn't know how many there were. Was Farouj missing because he was the killer, or was he just shacked up somewhere with a woman? Or did something much worse happen to him?

I never did find any other clients or husbands, so I might not even know the killer. I didn't even know who the schoolteacher was.

By now it was after midnight, and Karey had to get to get home. I waved for the bill and asked for a cab for her. Maybe we'd go shopping when this nightmare was over.

I signed the charge and headed up to bed. I'd be hungover tomorrow.

# Chapter Twelve

DeShane wasn't answering his phone. That worried me because we had an appointment in a half-hour. I was running late and wanted to ask if we could postpone until after I saw the probate lawyer. Everything was so screwed up by the missing will.

DeShane should be there. How can I disappoint him if he's not there?

I put my cellphone back in my pocket and stopped walking. I was at the locks where the boats waited to be raised to the canal's height before sailing off into the wilderness of Montague and Perth. It was a pretty sight with all of the brightly colored sailboats against the rough gray stone.

I was convinced that the missing student was guilty and probably ran back to his parents. I didn't remember which country they were all from, and I didn't have an excuse to go ask.

I wondered if Seline would know, since she saw them every month for their rent.

I still had reservations about Mr. Patel, too. Oh, I knew it was probably just that he didn't like me, but he had a depth of resentment I'd rarely seen. Not that he was unjustified; Snapper had abused him terribly with those contracts he'd signed. But was he angry enough to kill?

I needed to come up with a plan.

Then the whistle sounded, the lock started filling up with water, and everyone busied themselves getting ready. I was amazed at how quickly the canal filled.

And then the boats were on their way, jostling for position like toddlers at a birthday party.

I glanced at my watch. Three-fifteen. Well, Lord love a duck, I was late to my appointment with DeShane. Where did the time go?

I turned and hurried along the street. I still wanted to meet up about Bee's will. How was everything going to work?

To be honest, right now I wasn't ready to go through all of Aunt Bee's things and send them to the people she'd left them to. I wasn't ready to stay in the house either but with everything still locked in probate, I couldn't afford to stay at the hotel any longer.

Jaqi had a meeting in Ottawa with her publisher that she couldn't blow off, so Lucia and I would be on our own for the next few days. Not that we needed Jaqi here, it was just more fun with all three Musketeers.

As I neared the corner of Brockville and Main, I heard tires squeal. Looking back, I saw a car jump the curb and race toward me on the sidewalk. The sunshade was down, and the driver was wearing a hood or hat. I couldn't even make out their gender.

They flew toward me as I stood there, until it finally penetrated my thick skull.

They were trying to hit me.

I broke into a run, well, as much as I could run in these heels. Blast my vanity for dressing up to meet a good-looking man, even if I wasn't interested in him.

I turned the corner a little fast and wobbled on one heel. Grabbing the light post to stop my falling, I felt the heel snap.

My momentum tried to spin me around the pole, but I was too ungainly and only one foot hit the ground.

I dropped my purse to grab for support, but it was too late. I crashed against the cement base of the light post. My glasses went flying, I felt the rough cement scrape my cheek and the sidewalk take a layer of skin from my palm and knees.

I heard the car roar past on the street and looked up to see a black jeepish thing take the corner too fast.

I just sort of crouched there for a minute, winded and shocked.

"I'm okay," I whispered, more to myself than anything. I pulled myself up to a sitting position and did a reality check. My fancy red pump was broken; I'd have to walk barefoot. My nylons were torn to shreds, so bare legged as well.

Blood oozed from my knees and my right palm. I performed a brief internal check and while I stung where I'd scraped the skin off and felt bruised in a few places, nothing was broke but my bank account.

"C'mon Vee, get up and stop looking like a rag doll." I took off my one usable shoe and stuffed the broken heel into it. Then with both shoes in my left hand, I carefully stood up.

The weight of my bag, little though it was, kept me slightly off-balance. I only realized that I'd hit my head when blood started running into my eyes. I had to get cleaned up and checked out.

I could see an ambulance and a cop car flashing their lights halfway up the block. Perfect, I only had to imitate a hobbled zombie for about twenty yards.

As I neared the ambulance, I couldn't help but see that it was parked right in front of DeShane's office building.

"Oh no, not again." I closed my eyes to rub blood off of my forehead and saw Mr. Snapper lying on the floor again. I shook my head; there was no way that two of my lawyers were killed in the same week. The odds were one in... well, a lot.

But as the men in hospital uniforms pushed a stretcher up the bank from the canal my heart stopped.

Without thinking, I rushed over. A sheet covered the wet body, showing a dark figure underneath. Was I a Typhoid Mary for lawyers? Jaqi would be so upset.

I was about to say something when a hand grabbed me by the elbow. The bruised one.

"Well, now lookee here. A body is found and see who shows up looking like she's been a fight."

*No, no, no.* But as I turned toward the voice, I saw the sunburned and victorious face of Squinty MacGuinty. I swear that if it weren't for bad luck, I'd have no luck at all.

He had the nerve to grin as he asked me what truck did I get run over by? His grammar was as bad as his investigation.

His eyebrows lowered, and his bottom lip stuck out as his face reddened. I would have to learn not to think out loud before my mouth got me put in jail.

Water dripped from the gurney, leaving a puddle on the sidewalk as the attendants waited for MacGuinty to dismiss them.

He was too busy looking me up and down. His brow furrowed as a thought struggled its way to his mouth.

"What the hell happened to you?"

*Oh, by my pretty floral bonnet, I almost forgot.* "Someone just tried to kill me." I felt myself start to shake and tears burned my eyes. "They tried to run me over; didn't you see me at the corner?"

My voice moved up until only dogs could hear me as tears dripped down my cheeks.

I could feel the shift in his mood, before he awkwardly reached out to hug me. I stiffened in shock, and he released me.

"I'm sorry," I whispered. "I fell and twisted..."

He nodded and looked past me to the ambulance guys.

"Hey, Joe. You wanna take a look at a live one?"

Joe came over, giving MacGuinty a steady look before turning to me.

"Can you come over to the truck? I'd like to look at that head wound."

I nodded and followed him over. I was still a bit weirded out by that hug and wished Miko was here.

"So, Miss?"

"Lilley, Victoria Lilley."

A grin flashed over his face and was gone. "Alright, Miss Bond, how did you get these injuries?"

"I fell against the light-post. A car was chasing me." I paused as my heart sped up again. Someone had actually tried to kill me.

I tuned out the EMT's questions as I reflected on that. Someone, the killer, thought I knew more than I did. But I had no clue who they were. Well, technically, I had lots of clues, but they all pointed to different people.

Who had I spoken to recently? Seline, Mr. Patel, MacGuinty saw my lists. I squinted at him, but he just didn't seem smart enough to get away with murder. Though he was in a perfect position to pin it on someone else. My eyes narrowed; he'd tried hard enough to pin it on me.

I was distracted from my thoughts as The EMT clapped my shoulder and proclaimed himself finished. I touched my face. There were strips of tape holding the cut on my forehead closed, and a gauze bandage where I'd scraped my cheek on the light-pole base.

I thanked him and stood up so they could maneuver the stretcher inside.

I walked up to MacGuinty to ask if I could see the body. My neck felt cold at the thought of DeShane lying there, but I owed it to him to look.

MacGuinty pulled back the sheet showing a ravaged body, he had clearly been in the water for days.

It wasn't DeShane, I'd talked to him yesterday. Relief made my knees weak.

"I don't know him." He had a hooked nose, black, straight hair and a bullet hole between his eyebrows. He looked vaguely familiar.

"I wonder if this is Farouj." I turned to MacGuinty, "You know, Fadi's brother."

"Who is this fatty?"

"Fadi, with a D. He's one of the dozen or more students living on the third floor of Snapper's office building. He reported his brother missing days ago."

"Missing persons is not homicide." But he gazed thoughtfully at the body.

"It seems to be homicide now. Farouj was last seen heading off to class the morning of Mr. Snapper's demise."

"Was he now?" MacGuinty pulled at his lower lip. "But Snapper was stabbed."

I rolled my eyes. Only serial killers had a habit of using the same method on everyone they killed. "Maybe the building was too crowded for a gunshot at nine in the morning."

He nodded at me, I thought, but the ambulance guys grabbed the gurney and rolled poor Farouj into the back.

I heard a weird warbling noise from my pocket. I reached in and pulled out my phone. The screen was cracked, and I could see a bit of metal where the two halves had come apart at the seam.

Well, shit. I needed a new phone.

The drunk warbling sounded again, though the screen remained black. So, I answered it.

"Vee where have you been? You're almost an hour late; my next client is due in a few minutes."

It was Des. Thank all the Gods that ever were.

Apparently, my mic was damaged too, but I managed to get him downstairs. He probably heard me yelling into the phone from his open window.

After everything was explained, and he checked out my injuries, DeShane made certain MacGuinty was going to look into my near-death experience. Then he hurried to meet a man just arriving at the building.

I walked over to Mr. Patel's store, thinking he might carry cheap phones.

I hurt everywhere by now and was definitely cabbing back to the hotel the instant I had a working phone.

Not to mention I looked like disaster. I hated being seen like this.

I passed a small boutique and, even though I couldn't afford to, I bought a pair of jeans, sneakers and a nice blouse. I normally wasn't fond of casual jeans with a stylish top, but this was an emergency. I changed there and headed to the office. It was now *The Office* in my mind.

By the time I got there, I was limping and winded. I knew I should call Luci, but Jaqi had the car in Ottawa. All Luci could do was worry, so I didn't call.

The police tape was down, puddled on the stairs outside the store. It didn't look like the police had removed it—more like it had been torn away. Though by human hands or the wind, I had no idea. Possibly by Mr. Snapper's ghost.

A cold breeze ruffled the hair at the back of my neck, and I shivered. I decided to grab a go-cup of hot tea.

I sat on the bench in the faux marble entrance to catch my breath. The ribs on my left side must have hit the post; they were starting that bone-deep ache that made it hard to breathe.

Well, I couldn't sit here all day, so I lurched to my feet and went back into the store. I was right, Patel not only carried phones, he had pay-as-you-go and prepaid plans. And pretty, sparkley cases. I got a cheap folding phone and put ten dollars' worth of minutes on it. I would buy a proper one from my cell company. In the meantime, I put a purple jelly-case on it.

Now I felt human.

So, what next? Go home? Buy painkillers? Hide until the scabs go away?

I snorted, I was finishing what I'd started, that's what I was doing.

I decided to call Seline to see what she knew about Farouj. Then realized that her number was in my broken phone. Well, the office phone number was likely to be on the office door upstairs ,and Seline might have had the calls sent to her phone.

I turned and went out the lobby door and up the stairs. The old fire doors were heavy to pull open, and I was a more than a bit winded when I reached the second floor.

I should've used the elevator, but I was too impatient. Maybe Jaqi's fitness plan would work for me, too. What didn't work for me was bruised ribs and a flight of stairs.

I paused in the lobby until my breathing quieted. I could hear the clink of metal and the swish sound of papers being riffled through.

I smiled, Seline was here. How handy was that?

It didn't sound like packing up his papers though, it sounded like she was looking for something. But what? I already had my probate going through with a different lawyer. There must be other wills still not settled. But surely other lawyers had been hired for those cases too.

I tiptoed over; glad that I was wearing my new red sneakers, so my steps were silent. I adored my River Song low-heel pumps, but not for sleuthing.

I eased my eyes around the door, I know that sounds terribly wrong, but I wanted to see what she was up to.

Seline was squatting on her high heels in front of the opened safe. Her skirt had climbed almost to her nether regions, and I briefly envied the long slim slope of thigh. I knew that if I was squatting like that, I'd tip over onto my butt the first time I tried to move.

Seline was far more graceful when she reached into the back of the safe and pulled out a stack of photos. I couldn't see what was on them from here, and she quickly stuffed them into the box beside her.

I knocked quietly. She squawked and fell on her shapely butt. Just as clumsy as me. This pleased me for some reason that was definitely not pettiness.

She glared at from the floor, "What do you want?"

I moved to help her up, and she glared harder.

"I just wanted to know if you had heard about Farouj, the student upstairs."

As she stood, dusting herself off, I noticed my heart beating a little rapidly. Her perfume seemed too sweet and cloying. Why was I so nervous? Was I having a stroke?

No, the symptoms weren't right. Maybe it was my lizard brain reacting to something I haven't yet noticed.

But what?

I realized that Seline had called my name a few times and was now looking what my granny would call stroppy. Not quite looking for a fight, but not *not* looking for one either.

"Hello?" She waved her hand in front of my face. "Is anyone home?"

I smiled and tried to look sheepish.

"Sorry, I'm a bit distracted. I'm so sorry about that boy, and his brother must be devastated."

"What boy?" She asked, her eyes narrowed.

"The boy from upstairs, the missing one. The police found him this afternoon."

She paled a little. Then shrugged. "What's that to me?"

Clearly, she hadn't heard. I placed my hand on her shoulder. "Seline, the boy, Farouj, was found in the canal. He's dead."

She just shrugged again, but I kept my hand where it was. She must be in shock; she couldn't really be this heartless.

"We should go see Fadi," I said. "He's Farouj's brother."

She pushed my hand away.

"I'm too busy. I need to get everything sorted and cleaned out."

"That must be hard after working with him so long. I guess it makes his death real."

She looked at me with little lines forming between her brows.

"His death was real when you killed him." But there was no heat in her voice; I could tell she didn't believe her own words.

So why did she say them? And why was that itch back? What had I missed?

Never mind, it was time I got to the point of my visit. I scratched the back of my head, then forced my hand down.

"Seline, my new lawyer says that the estate paperwork hasn't arrived yet. I was wondering when..."

"I mailed them already. What do you want from me?"

She turned back to the safe and yanked the box closer. I could see a couple of the photos she'd thrown in. The top one was a naked man! It was a middle-aged woman with a very young man in the throes of, well, what people throe.

Why would Snapper have that in his safe?

Just as I realized why people have pictures of other people having sex in their safe—the pictures were in the safe, not the people, just to be clear—Seline turned to glare at me again.

I saw the dawning realization in her face, as she must've seen it in mine.

And just to put the cherry on top, I realized why her brooch was so familiar.

It was Bee's.

I turned and raced for the stairs before she could get up and go after me. I needed to get hold of Miko.

# Chapter Thirteen

I ran until I was sweaty. *Yuck.* I just knew my face was red from the way I huffed and puffed, bent over like an old woman.

*Hush, sixty is not old.*

I had to look around to see where I ended up and felt relieved to be on Main Street. There were a good number of people around, so I should be safe.

I needed to call Miko.

I needed to sit down.

More importantly, I needed to tinkle.

The Bun Journee was only a block or two away, so I hurried in that direction. The combination of too much tea and joggling my bladder while trying to run like Usain Bolt (Wasn't he well named?) had me wriggling in my jeans like a schoolgirl.

I pushed the door open and flew past Ben, shouting, "Phone Miko, it's an emergency!"

I'll never wear another pair of pants with a button fly again. It took forever undo all those cute little buttons. *Oh, who am I kidding!* These jeans were way too adorable. I knew I'd wear them again.

After splashing some cool water on my face, I went back to the seating area and waved Ben over.

"Oh, hun. I just had the scariest moment in my life. I know who the killer is. I need to talk to Miko."

But Miko was in court all day testifying. What was I going to do?

I had to talk it over with Luci. She had a good head for—well, good enough. Jaqi was the one with common sense, but I wasn't going to call Ottawa and interrupt her contract negotiations. Especially on a pay-as-you-go phone.

Ben grabbed me a cup of toasted almond coffee and a raspberry muffin to calm my nerves.

I didn't need more caffeine making me jumpy, but I drank it anyway. I needed to think. And I do that best out loud.

I tried calling Luci, but it went to voicemail. She was probably talking to Jaqi. I was bursting to tell someone.

"Ben, somebody tried to run me over this morning and then they found Farouj dead, the missing student near DeShane's office."

He dropped his teacup, spilling the last mouthful across the table. I leaped back as he grabbed a handful of napkins to wipe it up. Hey, these were hundred- and fifty-dollar jeans. I was not getting any tea stains the first time I wore them.

I was stalling, I knew it, but I just couldn't think about it long without getting cold sweats. And that wasn't a good look for me.

Ben apologized as he gave the table a last swipe. He watched me, eyes wide.

"Did you say—"

"Someone tried to kill me, yes. But that's not the worst part."

"There's a worse part? Vee, what's going on?"

I shook my head, was he not paying attention? Had we even met? Even Aunt Bee's neighbors knew I'd been looking into Mr. Snapper's murder.

So, I reminded him and started telling him about Bee's broach.

"Vee, please. Start at the beginning. My head is spinning."

I laid out my day: running late, calling Des to postpone, the locks, the jeep that tried to run me over, followed by poor Farouj's body, and finally, Miss Pineault and Aunt Bee's pin.

Ben got up without a word and fetched more coffee.

Back at the table, he scrubbed his hands through his hair, making it stand up like a Japanese cartoon character.

"Okay, Vee this is bad...way more than just regular bad."

I nodded; I knew that. "She knows I know. MacGuinty won't believe me; he still thinks it had to be a man to drive the letter opener into Snapper's chest like that."

I pushed my coffee away, too much caffeine and too much anxiety made my stomach burn.

"But if she knew what she was doing and slid it between the ribs..." I paused, not wanting to picture it.

"Okay, okay'" Ben's voice was shaky. "Did she follow you?"

I shook my head. If she'd followed me, she'd have caught me after the first block.

"So, what is she doing now?"

I felt my face pale. She wouldn't still be sitting in the office; she'd have to think I called the police.

What did she know about me?

Everything. I dug out my new phone to call Lucia to tell her to hide somewhere, maybe meet me here, but there was no answer. It went to voicemail again. I called the room directly, but it just rang and rang, eventually turning over to another voicemail.

"Luci, if you get this, please stay in the room. Don't let anyone in. I figured it out but now she's—well, just stay in the room."

Seline Pineault. The slick, sexy secretary, emphasis on the secret. She had swindled Aunt Bee. I couldn't prove it was her yet, but I just knew it.

Oh yeah. My new estate lawyer had heard from the bank at long last, Bee's accounts were nearly empty.

That probably meant that poor Mr. Snapper caught her,and she'd killed him. Bee probably died from the stress of her money disappearing from her bank.

"Well, she isn't going to get away with it. Not if I have anything to do with it."

"Me too. You are not facing this alone. I'll help cover your twelve."

I smiled even as I shook my head no. "That's *cover your six*, sweetie."

"But there are two of us, so it's twelve." He grinned.

"Ben, I know you want to help, but I refuse to put you in danger. Miko would kill me. You stay here and call the police if I'm not back or don't call you by six. Tell them everything."

He opened his mouth to object, but I shook my head firmly. "This is my task, my revenge for Bee."

I would have to call Jaqi now. Not that she'd be back in time to do anything, and she would be panicked while trying to drive back. But if things didn't work out, I didn't want it to blindside her.

I prayed that Luci was on the phone, that she was safe. My heart seemed to skip a couple of beats before speeding up to scary levels. My blood whooshed in my ears and my voice sounded hollow.

"She's got Luci."

I wasn't confident in my ability to fight, though I might have a structural advantage, big hands and all. I needed someone waiting by the phone to call in the experts if things went badly.

That's where Ben came in.

Oh, I wasn't clueless to how foolish I acted, I just needed to look in her eyes and ask if it was worth it. Was all the killing and all the misery worth it?

"Ben, what if Luci is already dead and Seline is sitting there, waiting for me to get back?"

"Don't think like that. Call her again."

I did but this time was like the last six times. No answer. It wasn't like Lucia to talk this long on long distance. At the rates the cell phone company charged, she'd be texting Jaqi.

I hung up and stared at Ben's worried face.

"I should have left this up to the cops. What if I killed her?"

I started to sob. My too-fast heart beating throbbed louder than his reply. My neck was cold, and I felt both nauseated and faint. I was about to throw up.

Ben got up and gently pushed my head down. He brought me a wet cloth to put on the back of my neck. I felt better almost instantly.

At least physically. My heart was still pounding away like a kid with a new drum set. I thought about the bullet hole in Farouj's forehead. And about how Snapper was stabbed with something handy.

MacGuinty was right, the methods were polar opposites—one spur of the moment, one cold and calculated. But there weren't two killers. Were there? If so, which one grabbed Luci?

I only realized I spoke out loud again when Ben squeezed my hand.

He opened his mouth just as a group of teenagers pushed open the door and blew in like a scatter of leaves. They were laughing and heading to the counter when Ben stood up.

"I'm sorry, we're closed."

The tallest boy glowered at him, and then made a show of checking the sign on the door. "Not according to this."

But his girlfriend took one look at me and touched his arm, shaking her head.

"Let's go." The other girls stared at me and nodded. As the group drifted back out, I heard one mutter something about hysterical old lady, but I let it pass. They were right.

What had I done?

Ben flipped the sign and turned off the outside lights. Now it was really closed.

"I can't let you keep closing early. You'll lose business."

"Don't be silly. This is way more important."

But we just sat there staring at each other.

Finally, Ben said, "Two killers? Like Snapper killed the student then Seline killed him?"

I thought about it. Maybe. "Why, though? A love triangle? Seline wasn't sad; she wasn't scared like she thought there was a second killer. She was... annoyed at me."

"Annoyed?"

"Yes, like I was telling her something she already knew."

We stared at each other. Then Ben slowly stated, "She already knew."

"Yes, but no." I remembered her paling when I told her. "She wasn't upset that he was dead, she was upset that he was found."

"So, she did kill both."

"And now she has my best friend."

# Chapter Fourteen

I held my breath and called Jaqi. I told myself that it was just to see if she was on the phone with Lucia.

She wasn't. She answered on the first ring.

"Hey, Vee. Good timing, we're on a break."

"You're taking a break from lunch?"

Jaqi laughed the sound out of place in my fear. "No, it turned into a big meeting. Marketing guy, designer, everyone. They have big plans for my new series."

I smiled briefly. "That's great news, hun."

"Hun? You never call me that unless you're worried. What's going on?"

I held my breath, searching for the right words. I couldn't find any.

"I think Luci's missing."

"Did you check the local crystal shop?"

I hated to ruin her mood, but I told her everything. She was silent for a long time.

"I'm coming back."

"No, Jaqi, stay at your meeting, it's important."

"And Luci isn't?" Her voice hardened.

"That's not what I mean." I took a deep breath, pushing my emotions to the back of my mind. "Miko is going to help, and Ben and I have a plan." I crossed my fingers that she wouldn't realize how pathetic our plan was.

"Leave it to Miko, then. Stay out of it, Vee. You've done enough."

I swear I could hear my heart break when Jaqi hung up without another word.

I was jittery from too much coffee and my heart was beating way too fast, but we had a plan. Maybe. It's possible some of the nervousness was from worry.

I nearly jumped out of my skin when my cell rang. The noise seemed louder and strident in the silence.

I didn't recognize the number.

Ben reached over to hold my hand as I picked up the phone and pushed accept.

"Hello?"

"Miss Lilley? Vee." Seline's voice was sweet as maple flavored syrup and just as fake. I nodded at Ben; it was time. Too late to second guess anything. I took a deep breath and smiled.

"Hello, Seline. What's up?"

"Don't play with me. I have your bestie, and I'm already sick of her face."

I could hear Ben murmuring into his phone by the cash.

"Okay, what do you want?"

I glanced at Ben and he shook his head, Miko was still in court.

*Fiddlesticks!* I did not want to deal with Squinty MacGuinty when it was this important. I shrugged at Ben, what else was there to do?

"I want you to come to my office. I give you twenty minutes. Better jump, girl." She hung up.

That killed the first part of the plan, getting as much information for the cops as possible. And stalling her, of course, to give them a chance to get there.

I grabbed my purse and headed for the door. Ben called to me that MacGuinty was unavailable, too.

I yelled "Keep trying!" over my shoulder as I stepped out.

I was breathless after only one block. Fear and pain made my chest too tight to move quickly. Taking a couple of deep breaths, I ran again. Within a dozen yards ,I felt a stitch in my side. I had to stop.

"Think." I made myself calm down by sheer force of will. Seline wanted me too panicked to think and too tired from running to fight.

And she was at her office, so there must be something there she was still looking for.

I glanced at my watch, but it was pointless. I'd hadn't thought to check the time when Seline hung up. How much longer did I have?

*Think!* It was under fifteen minutes from the Bun Journee to the office anyway. And I'd run several blocks already. Okay, a few blocks. Two...I'd run two blocks. Most of two blocks.

That still put me ahead of her schedule. How could I use that to my advantage?

And where the H-E- double hockey sticks were all the cops in this town?

I made it to the corner of Brockville and Main quickly. I'd figured out that the jog-walk-jog method was fast enough and let me breathe.

*So, now what?* I called Ben to check on my police backup, but he still hadn't gotten through, and the jerk at the desk thought it was a prank call.

*Just me, then.* Well, that meant there was nobody to hold me back, right?

I stepped into the building and headed for the stairs.

LUCIA WAS TIED TO A chair with a gag in her mouth. I leaned in further, but Luci spied me and shook her head. She didn't want rescuing?

I pointed to myself, then to her. I would go untie her. She shook her head again then jerked it toward me and then sideways.

She wanted me to...*leave*? I mimed holding a phone and dialing. She nodded vigorously.

So, I did what she asked, though it broke my heart to leave her there. Her big, dark eyes looked haunted. She'd grown up in a terribly violent and poor neighborhood. Would that give her the edge she needed? Or would it trigger PTSD and make her lash out?

I hurried to the stairs and grunted as quietly as I could while pulling the heavy door across the thick carpet.

I tried to tug it shut behind me, but it stuck. A small area rug over the wall to wall carpet had bunched up. Yanking was useless, so I gave up and pulled out my cell.

I only dialed 9 and 1 when I heard a gentle throat clearing. I looked up, my heart falling. It was Seline and her enormous, huge and terrifying gun. How did such a feminine little thing carry such a big weapon? It should pull her off balance.

Could I take advantage of that?

She held out her hand for my phone and I pushed the last 1 as I handed it over. Of course, she checked the screen and closed the phone.

She gestured, waving the gun for me to return to the office. Luci slumped when she us come in and the frowning secretary holding my bright purple cell.

I shrugged; I had tried. I blamed the door for getting stuck on the carpet. Unbelievable, killed for a bloody door.

Seline looked around, and then pointed at the plain wooden chair I'd sat in for the reading.

"Drag that over beside your friend." She shoved my phone into her jacket pocket to point to the spot beside my best friend.

"Is the black one here, too? Should I put a sign on the stairs for her to come right up?" She laughed at her wit, we didn't.

As I did what she'd ordered me to, my heart sank. This is my fault. I should have trusted Miko.

"I'm out of rope, but if you move, I'll shoot your friend."

I wasn't going to die like this. Well, maybe, but I'd go out fighting or at least arguing.

As she moved back to the safe, I shifted myself to the edge of my chair. If I could free Luci's hands, we could both make a break for it.

"I said not to move."

Her voice was all the more menacing for being soft. "Sorry, Seline, I was just getting comfortable. I won't move again."

Damned woman had eyes in the back of her head. Of course, now I was sitting on the edge of the chair and it was pressing into my buttock. Just great.

I decided to ask all of the questions I hadn't figured out yet. Talking wasn't moving, after all.

"Um, Seline? Why are you doing this?"

She glanced back at me at me and shook her head, her perfect, blond hair swinging about her neck.

"Come on," I said. "What's the harm? It's not like there's anyone to tell."

"Where is Black Beauty anyway?"

"I glanced at Lucia and her eyes were flashing in ... anger? Jealousy?

"She's in Ottawa, she's late with her book."

"She's in trouble with the library?" Seline snorted with laughter. Luci shot me a meaningful glance, which I interpreted to mean don't correct her.

"She's very responsible." I muttered.

"Well," Seline grinned rather maniacally at me. "Since it's just us girls."

I smiled, trying not to look as scared as I felt.

She turned back to the safe. "Do you have any idea how much it costs to become a paralegal?" Her words sounded hollow. How poetic. "A lot. And this jerk tells me he needs a proper paralegal but only gives me secretarial work. And too little pay to get rid of my student loans."

"That's pretty harsh. I had a boss like that once, always an excuse." I sympathized. *We're on her side until she unties us, right?*

She muttered an expletive that I assumed meant she agreed with me. Remembering catching her and Snapper in *flagrente delecto* as it were, I decided to add another layer to our bonding. I just hoped she was bonding with me. If she played me the way I played her... no, I wouldn't even think it.

"My last boss was a real playboy, at least he thought he was. Tried to force the performers to sleep with him. No sex, no prime slot. You end up at 6:00 p.m. before the audience arrives, or at midnight after they leave."

Seline leaned on one hand to peer at me. "You were a stripper?" She looked pretty doubtful.

"No, can you picture me as an exotic dancer?" I let out a strangled laugh. "I was a drag queen—when I was much younger, of course. I wore bright green contacts and too much concealer. I was glorious."

She stared for a moment, then said, "Huh," and went back to pilfering the safe.

"Of course, I was hit on all the time, both by the club manager and customers. I swear he told them I was easy...just to punish me for not...you know."

Just then Lucia made a strangled noise and without thinking, I turned and yanked the gag out of her mouth. She sputtered and coughed for the few moments it took our captor to come over to stand in front of us. Luci was pale and beads of sweat dotted her hairline.

Seline moved to put the gag back, but Luci shook her head no.

"Por favor, I can't breathe. I have the asthma. I'll be good, I promise."

After a long moment, Seline nodded and hurried back to her work.

I hadn't known Lucia had asthma. Was it dangerous? Could it kill her? I turned to her, scared I couldn't talk our way out in time. She was grinning, and perfectly fine. How had she looked so sick a moment ago?

But I couldn't ask so I went back to charming Seline out of killing us. Or trying to.

"Mr. Snapper seemed the same type of man as my boss at the club, handsy, no means push harder. That sort."

She nodded, glancing back at us. Her movement upset her precarious balance and she almost toppled over.

"At least tell me how you stole Aunt Bee's money. And her jewelry. And if you killed the student."

She pulled herself off the floor with the aid of the desk and stared at me.

"You're just figuring that out now? Why did you even come here?"

I shrugged. "I thought the guy with the teacher-wife killed Mr. Snapper. I came to see if you knew anything that could prove it. Or at least knew his name."

She stared at me for a full twenty seconds before dissolving in laughter. I smiled back. Maybe she'd let us go if she thought I was senile.

No luck. As she wiped her tears with one hand, she pointed the gun at us with the other.

"I'm so sorry, but that's hilarious. You came to me for help." She pulled herself together and her eyes hardened. "You can stop trying to chat me up, it won't work."

I slumped. Now what was I to do?

Lucia leaned as far over as she could, bending at the waist and coughing. I put my arm over her shoulder, hugging her to me.

"Untie me." Her voice was so soft, I barely heard it. *She was faking!*

I checked what Seline was doing, and she seemed to be ignoring Luci's asthma attack. It sounded real, too; I wondered briefly if Luci was faking it. But I pushed that aside and slipped my left hand down to her bound wrists.

They were securely tied. At least a triple knot.

*Well, shit on a sandwich.*

SELINE PINEAULT: THIEF, liar, and killer. Now kidnapper. And to think I had loved her shoes.

Well, no more. Her shoes were dead to me. Well, maybe not the red pair.

But I still had questions.

Like why did she kill Farouj, and where could I get my jacket dry-cleaned in Smiths Falls? Also, why did she kill her boss?

I suppose that last one was the most important question. If only she hadn't taken my phone.

Wait, did Lucia still have her phone? I was through two of the knots binding her wrists; all that time doing magic tricks for beer was finally paying off.

Then Luci started coughing again, harder, her face turning bright red. I started pounding on her back which just made her redder. Her breathing was ragged and her eyes teared.

My heart was in my throat. My hands shook as I levered myself to my feet.

Seline looked up from the floor in front of the safe where she was sorting through envelopes.

"Don't try it." Her voice was flat, cold. Far scarier than when she'd yelled at me earlier.

"I'm just getting some water for Lucia, the cooler's right outside this door. You can watch me."

She stood and moved toward the door until she could see the lobby.

"Okay, get her a drink but be quick about it. I don't have much time left."

I nodded and rushed out as fast as the pins and needles in my left leg would let me.

I grabbed a cup off of her desk and turned to the cooler. I caught a glimpse of movement by the stairway door, but I tried not to react. It didn't matter; Luci's safety was my only concern.

I hurried to Lucia's side, noticing that her head was resting on the chair back, her chest heaving with the difficulty of breathing. Even Miss Pineault looked a bit worried.

Seline said nothing as I hurried over to gently lift Luci's head and held the cup at her lips. Luci sipped then shook her head. I sat beside her, keeping a good eye on her breathing. Pineault nodded and went back to the safe. What was she looking for?

So, it wasn't my fault that it took me several minutes to notice that Luci had completely escaped her rope and was now just holding it in her hands.

I glanced over at the evil seductress. Had she seduced poor Snapper into her deadly game?

I didn't know any more now than I had yesterday. Well, I knew who killed my lawyer. At least I think I did. I didn't really want to ask. Ignorance might not be bliss, but it was probably safer. Safe being a relative concept.

Luci cleared her throat, and I looked over. She had one end of the rope in each hand, like she was going to strangle someone. Maybe she would, she was pretty steamed about poor Victor's cracked rib.

I heard a grunt from behind the desk, like someone picked up something tremendously heavy. Luci nudged my shoulder. Showtime.

Tiptoeing like cartoon characters, we managed to get around the back of the desk before a sound in the lobby brought Miss Pineault's head up like a snake rearing up to bite your privates. She saw us immediately and reached for the gun.

I threw myself between Luci and the gun, twisting my right knee. I lurched to the side, knocking Luci against the desk and making her miss her attempt to grab Seline's arm with her rope.

Then the room was filled with cops and the gun went off. The last thing I heard was Luci scream.

# Chapter Fifteen

I woke up slowly, an incessant beeping annoying me back to life. I had to struggle to get my eyes open. It felt like they were crazy glued shut. I reached up to wipe them, but my arm was stiff. It wouldn't bend.

I felt positive I was dead. They glue your eyes shut for the funeral, after rigor mortis had set in. I gasped for breath—was I breathing?

A soft hand touched mine, and I heard Luci's voice murmur at me. Oh, my Lord, was she dead too? Crushed by guilt, I bereated myself for not leaving it all to the cops. Now who would mourn Aunt Bee? Or me, for that matter? Jaqi would hate me for getting her lover killed.

Soon, a soft, damp cloth washed my eyes, and I opened them to Luci's worried frown. I blinked a few times, but she was still there.

Jaqi leaned into view behind her. They were smiling. I meant to ask if we were all okay, but my throat cracked and croaked. What was that horrible noise, it couldn't be me.

Lucia quickly turned to pick up a glass of water and pressed the straw to my lips. It was glorious, the best water I've ever tasted. I could almost hear it sizzling against my hot, dry throat. Okay, I must be alive.

I didn't realize that I'd spoken out loud until Luci nodded, smiling.

"Of course, you are. You're the hero."

"I'm what? What happened?" My mind was stubbornly blank, I remembered nothing that was heroic or would end with me in a hospital.

Jaqi sent Lucia to get the nurse and leaned over to hug me. There were tears in her eyes.

"You stupid, fucking idiot." She was holding on really hard to be whispering those words. It just confused me more.

"Too tight," I whispered, and she eased up. "What happened?"

"You don't remember? You got shot."

Shot?" I squeaked, my throat tightening.

"You tried to hit her, and the gun went off. Don't you remember?"

I shook my head slowly. That sounded so unlike me. I'm not a violent person. Nosy and pushy, yes, but not violent.

Jaqi patted my hand, "Luci can tell you. She was there."

Just then the nurse stepped in, quickly followed by a doctor and a beaming Lucia. I was definitely alive. The brisk examination proved it. I yelped with pain when the doctor removed the blanket to examine my right hip.

"Doesn't look too bad. You're a lucky woman. The bullet shattered part of your hip but missed your femoral artery."

I nodded like I knew what he was talking about.

"We'll keep you for a couple days to see how it's healing," he continued, "but you could be home for the weekend."

I heard Luci squeal, quickly shushed by Jaqi.

After the medical peeps left, I stared Luci straight in the eye and put on my most no-nonsense face. "Okay, spill it. What happened?"

As she talked, vague memories surfaced, and I realized how very lucky we were. I opened my mouth to apologize for putting her in so much danger, but what came out was, "I hope that shut the frigging, sleaze-ball cop up."

Jaqi smiled at me. "No, but he said he might have made a mistake, an honest one. It was brilliant of you to dial 911 and leave the line open, the operator got the whole thing on tape."

*Fabulous, now everyone in town knows I used to be a drag queen.*

I HAD COME BY AMBULANCE with nothing but my purse and the clothes I was wearing. How did I get enough stuff to need a duffel bag?

Luci, that's how. She'd brought a few things each time she visited, first a comfy nightie and slippers, then my hairbrush and toothbrush, and books, a small potted rosebush, a nice blouse and sweater...the list went on.

As I pushed to get the last article into the pretty pink bag, I was glad that I'd only been here a few days. Another week, and I'd need a truck to take my things home.

I heard a tap at the door and someone clearing their throat behind me.

"I'm almost finished," I said. "Who knew it would be so hard to pack a few things from a wheelchair?"

"Fr—Victoria?"

I spun myself around, and it wasn't Carol, my nurse.

It was my mother.

I settled myself deeper into my chair. It wasn't as supportive as the girls would be, but hopefully they'd be here soon.

My mother cleared her throat again, and I waved for her to come in. Unsurprisingly, she shut the door behind her.

Right. I just had to get through the next few minutes without losing my temper. As soon as the will was settled, I'd happily estrange her. *Doesn't that sound so much classier than cut her out of my life?*

Then it really hit me she was standing there. In my room. "Wait. What?"

"Honestly, if you don't list—" She took a deep breath. "Victoria, I'm sorry. I should have listened to you when you told me Sean was railwaying you into prison."

"Railroading."

She grimaced and continued as if she hadn't heard me. "I knew Sean inherited his father's mean streak, but his mother was—" She shook her head, and I noticed that her hair was loose instead of being pulled up into a severe bun.

In fact, she looked downright disheveled. Her sweater didn't match her pants, and there was a tea stain on her shirt. We didn't always see eye to eye, well never, but whoever had her in this state would be dead.

"What happened? Did Squinty MacGuinty say something to you?"

She smiled briefly and shook her head again.

"No, Victoria, I did it to myself. Always so worried about what people would think. You know what, they don't think at all."

She dashed her sleeve across her eyes, smearing the mascara and leaving a black smudge on her butter-colored cardigan.

"Mom?" She leaned over to grasp my hand and held it tight.

"Fr—Victoria, I am so sorry about how I've behaved. Skipping your wedding...no, I hated that man the first time I met him. But the way I've treated you...I can never make up to you."

"Are you serious? Where is my real mother?"

"I don't blame you. I just wish I'd come to my senses before you nearly died."

"It's okay, Mom. Honestly. I'm just glad you're..." *What? Sane now? Accepting me at last?* "Here."

She pulled me forward for a hug, and I whimpered as the pain from my hip rocketed up to my ribs.

My mother paled as she realized what she'd done, then she reached for the call button.

"No, I'm okay. I want to go home, and they'll want to keep me if they think I'm still in pain."

She nodded.

"What provoked this sudden and total change?"

"I thought I'd killed you. When Lucia called to tell me you'd been shot by the real murderer, I just..."

She trailed off but her expression said it all. Fear, guilt, horror, self-recrimination, fear... I repeated the word on purpose because she was so clearly frightened. "I've already told the other police officer that we were lying about you being cut from the will. I don't know why I let them talk me into saying that in the first place."

"So, is Miss Pineault behind bars?"

Mom nodded. "She's not admitting anything, but she was caught red-handed. Lucia says that you caught her."

I nodded now, though I hadn't meant to get taken hostage by Seline.

"They were stealing Aunt Bee blind. Her bank accounts, her investments, even the jewelry from her bank box. They thought she was just a lonely old woman and tried to take everything from her."

I felt tears roughen my voice. "She never admitted killing Aunt Bee to me either, though she did admit to everything else when she thought she'd get rid of us. I guess villains really do need to brag to someone. Maybe Bee did just die of old age." My voice whispered to a halt.

The door flew open and Lucia strode in, her face set in lines of anger.

"You"—she pointed to my mother—"Get out and leave her alone. Vee nearly died; this is no time for your puritan-shaming and deadnaming."

That was when I realized that my mother had been calling me Victoria during this visit. As I hastened to assure the girls that everything was fine, I couldn't help but smile. It felt so good to be accepted as who I was.

My mom ignored them and tapped my shoulder gently, "Victoria is such a mouthful Mind if I call you Vicky?"

The girls and I all said "No!" in unison.

THREE WEEKS LATER...

Jaqi and Lucia were helping me sort through Aunt Bee's belongings. There were some things I'd give to others in my family, some to her friends, and some to charity. I'd keep most of my legacy, especially her beautiful antique furniture, but you know how it goes. Not everything suited my tastes.

So, I'd set up an online auction through one of those antique companies, and all of the income was going to a struggling LGBT outreach that had lost some of its government funding. I'd had DeShane set me up a not-for-profit company while I was still in hospital. The last thing I wanted was for my name to be on this. Or at least not to be easily found. *Can you imagine the number of people who would come out to beg for money?*

Anyway, the girls had dragged one of Bee's velvet rockers into the driveway and made me swear to stay sitting. I didn't mind, it was one of the pieces I was keeping. Dark blue velvet and Louis XV trim hid a modern lounger. I loved it.

My hip was healing as well as one might expect. I would need a walker or cane for the next few months, but I assumed it would eventually heal up. Right now, walking was white hot sheets of pain, but the sadists in the physio department made me swear to exercise and walk at least five-thousand steps a day. I wanted lie and say I did but two things stopped me: I try to always honor my promises and I'm an ethical woman.

And Jaqi bought me one of those watches that count your steps, your heart rate and so on, then send it to your computer. Or in this case, Jaqi's computer.

Anyway, today we'd tackle the garage. It was a two-car garage; one half had her beautiful car hiding in its heavy cotton cover. The other was storage and a work area. I was surprised to see power tools and compressors and things. Bee had never seemed to be very handy, but then I knew little of her youth.

Jaqi carefully pulled some of the car's cover off and gasped at the deep red paint and the heavy chrome. Luci stepped over and squealed.

"We must drive this. Just a bit, to be sure it's working."

"I know," I said. "We'll need to check it over first. I'm not ruining Bee's car because it needs oil."

They grinned at me, a bright light shining in both sets of dark brown eyes. I couldn't help grinning back.

Lucia pulled the car cover from Jaqi's hands and laid it back carefully.

"Let us hurry up and finish so we can go riding in the car."

A short time later, I heard Jaqi whistle. They were in the back of the storage side, so I couldn't see what she'd found. Not even twisting in my seat helped. I started to lever myself up, but my hip shrieked like a banshee with the pain.

I saw Jaqi and Luci running my way and realized that it had actually been me shrieking. I waved them back, feeling embarrassed.

"Don't worry about me, what did you find?"

Jaqi pulled at her lip, assessing me, then nodded.

"I'm not sure what it's called these days, but it looks like a gypsy wagon. It needs a little TLC, and a paint job but..."

"A vardo. Bee had Roma blood."

My cell phone shrilled, nearly giving me a heart attack. I had to figure out how to change that ringtone. It was an unlisted number. Odd.

"Hello?"

"Miss Lilley, it's Miko Shiomi."

I waved the girls off. "It's Miko, the cute cop." I expected him to react to that, but he sounded so serious when he did reply.

"Miss Lilley, I thought you should know that we got the tox results back from Beatrice Lilley's autopsy."

"Do I really want to hear this? I'd rather not picture her being taken apart like a puzzle. Besides, we already knew she died in her sleep."

"Vee, it wasn't a natural death. Someone poisoned her."

My lungs froze, and I couldn't breathe. I could hear my blood swishing through my ears. "What?!"

"She was poisone., Saint John's wort and dextromethorphan."

"Oh. She did use Saint John's Wort to help her sleep. Did she have a cold? It could've been an accident."

"Not in these amounts. I'm so sorry, but we're opening a homicide investigation. And since you inherited so much..." His voice trailed off.

"You are not calling to tell me I'm a suspect!" I hung up on him.

I couldn't believe it. My phone rang again with the same number, and I rejected the call. *Of all the nerve.* My anger faded fast, though. Poor Aunt Bee. Who would murder a ninety-four-year-old lady? She only had a couple years left; they could have just waited.

Sorrow swept through me, and I no longer wanted to think about Bee's stuff. I ignored the girls' questions and gestured for Luci to help me up.

<<<>>>

Delilah Knight is the fun, more colorful alter-ego of author Laurie Stewart. Delilah writes LGBT+ and senior cozy mysteries which are inclusive of gender, sexuality, race, age and ability. As Miss Vee says," if they want my money, they'd better be ready to include me."

Laurie Stewart writes speculative and paranormal novels and short stories and has been published in a number of anthologies. Her stories are also inclusive, but don't necessarily have the marginalized characters as the hero. The way Delilah does.

YOU CAN FOLLOW BOTH personalities on Facebook or on Laurie's blog.

www.delilahknight-author.com[1]
www.lauriestewart-author.com[2]

---

1.    http://www.delilahknight-author.com

2.    http://www.lauriestewart-author.com

# Don't miss out!

Visit the website below and you can sign up to receive emails whenever Delilah Knight publishes a new book. There's no charge and no obligation.

https://books2read.com/r/B-A-ZPJM-ZGAJB

**BOOKS 2 READ**

Connecting independent readers to independent writers.

# Also by Delilah Knight

**Miss Vee Mysteries**
Miss Vee and the Lecherous Lawyer

# About the Author

Delilah Knight is the fun, more colorful alter-ego of author Laurie Stewart. Delilah writes LGBT+ and senior cozy mysteries which are inclusive of gender, sexuality, race, age and ability. As Miss Vee says," if they want my money, they'd better be ready to include me."

Laurie Stewart writes speculative and paranormal novels and short stories and has been published in a number of anthologies. Her stories are also inclusive, but don't necessarily have the marginalized characters as the hero. The way Delilah does.

Read more at www.delilahknight-author.com.